CU00747021

The Girl on the Beach
And Other Stories

– MICHAEL JIMACK –

Printed and bound in England by www.printondemand-worldwide.com

http://www.fast-print.net/bookshop

THE GIRL ON THE BEACH
AND OTHER STORIES
Copyright © Michael Jimack 2016

ISBN 978-178456-421-6

First published 2017 by
FASTPRINT PUBLISHING
Peterborough, England.

Contents

The Girl on the Beach	5
Nostalgia	12
Ambition	18
An Old Man and a Tree	27
An Unlikely Friendship	33
Kinky Susan	40
The Quality of Mercy	47
Oh Mr Stanislavsky!	55
A Strange Portrait	63
A Piece of Chocolate	69
Mancurren	74
A Good Deed	82
An Eventful Day	94
The Blue Uniform	101
The Two Friends	110
A Railway Journey	119
Mr Know-All	125
Retribution	132
Could That Have Been Me?	141
Bob Briscoe's Dream Girl	148
Princess Zaza	154
A Fateful Meeting	166

The Girl on the Beach

M att came to a sudden halt. He had been running along the coastal path for the last half hour. He was not out of breath, he had developed a comfortable rhythm and could have continued for many more miles, but what made him stop was the stunning beauty of the scene before him. It was a little bay, secret and deserted. A gully in the cliff face led down to a shimmering white beach, so tropical a few windswept palms would not have been out of place. The sky was cloudless and a soft warm breeze brushed his face. The green-blue sea lapped the shore, gently surging forth and hissing back sleepily, awaking memories of happy childhood holidays on sunny beaches.

He had booked the cottage in Penryn for a week. His girlfriend had recently ended their relationship and he wanted to be on his own to think things over. Her parting words had stung him, but he had to admit there was something in what she had said.

"You are clever, but you're a dilettante, a grasshopper; you never stick with anything and you would rather be climbing or paragliding than concentrating on your career."

Now that the sun was well up the birds were silent, but a drone of insects filled the air. Matt sat on a rock and gazed out to sea; on the horizon a sail, just a faint speck, but when he shielded his eyes and looked again it was gone. He turned his attention to the little cove and, to his surprise a solitary figure emerged from the shadow of the cliff. It was a young woman in a cotton shift. She stood in the sunlight looking out to sea and then suddenly pulled the shift over her head and dropped it on the sand. She was completely naked. Even from his perch on the cliff top he could see she was beautiful. The girl walked slowly towards the sea.

Matt smiled; she was going to have a swim in this deserted place, he thought, and wondered where she came from. The girl immersed herself and started swimming directly out to sea. He sat watching, wondering when she would turn around and head for the shore, but she kept on going. Matt stood up; what was she doing? She was far out now and clearly not turning back. With a shock, it dawned upon him that she had no intention of turning back; she was going to swim until utterly exhausted, and let the ocean take her. She wanted to die.

He did not hesitate, but started clambering down the gully, sliding and slipping in his haste to get to the bottom. Pausing only to remove his shoes, he sprinted over the sand and plunged into the sea.

Matt was a strong swimmer and he headed out to where he had last seen a bobbing head. He kept up a steady stroke, his arms neatly slicing the water, but there was no sign of the girl. By this time he must have been nearly a mile offshore, and he was beginning to tire. He would have to turn around if he were not to get into difficulties himself. He gave one last look around him, but saw only the ripple and sparkle of the sun-kissed sea so, reluctantly, he headed for the beach. He padded towards the cliff-face and found his shoes. His shorts and tee-shirt would soon dry in the sun, but where was the girl's shift? He searched the sand and shoreline, but there was no sign of it. The breeze had strengthened - perhaps it had blown away. When he reported the matter, the police would send someone to look for it. By the time he had arrived back at his holiday cottage he was bone-dry. There were no police in the village and so he had to telephone the police station some twenty miles away. He told his story first to the desk sergeant and then to a detective, who arrived with a colleague thirty minutes later to begin their inquiries. It was apparent that the girl could not have come from far away, so they began their house-to-house by asking if a young woman had left home that morning and not returned. All were accounted for, and so they enlisted the services of a boatman to take them to the cove, this being the easiest way to get there. The only other access was via the rocky gully, although it was probably possible to get there at low tide by skirting all around the base of the sea cliffs. The two police officers searched for over an hour but found no trace of clothing, and they began to doubt the truth of Matt's account; only, what would be the point of making up a story like that? So they decided to call on him for the second time that day.

He was on the defensive when the older detective said,

"I am not saying that you deliberately made this up, but perhaps you imagined it. You had been running for some time, a dazzling glare reflected from the sea creating a heat haze and, if you were on any medication..."

He was struggling to find an explanation.

"I am very fit and not on any medication, and I resent your suggestion. Why don't you find out if she came from Tregoran? It's only five miles away and she could have walked from there, climbed down the gully and hidden her shoes under some stones."

"We'll look into that, of course," he said, backtracking, "But if nobody reports a young woman as missing, and nobody is washed up on the foreshore, there is little else we can do."

Matt was puzzled; the episode was very real to him. Could he have swum out to sea after a phantom? He didn't think so. He walked down to the harbour and into the local inn, the *Mariner's Arms*.

The barmaid, a good-looking young woman, smiled at him.

"Was it you who saw a girl swim out to sea?"

"Yes."

"And they say you tried to save her?"

He took a sip of his beer.

"That was brave of you."

She studied his physique.

"I'm a strong swimmer."

"Some folk here tell of a woman who walked into the sea because she didn't want to live. They heard it from their parents, who heard it from theirs, so it was a long time ago, the eighteen-nineties, I think."

She handed him a menu.

Why was she telling him that?

"It's sad, but these things happen," he said.

"Why don't you look into that story?" She bent forward over the bar counter, showing a lot of cleavage.

"Why would I do that?"

"Because it might throw some light on what you saw; history can repeat itself, you know."

The next day he phoned the police and was told that their enquiries at Tregoron had drawn a blank, and they would be taking no further action unless new facts came to light. He'd run along the cliff path again that morning and seen nothing unusual. The light was different because the sky was overcast, but the cove still had a mysterious beauty. For one heart-thumping moment he thought he saw the girl's shift lying on the shoreline at the far edge of the cove, but it was only a white rock.

He made some coffee and stared out of the window. The barmaid had said he should look into that old tragedy. Why not? He had nothing better to do; he would consult the county records, and see what he could find out. On the drive inland he thought about his ex-girlfriend's parting shot. Perhaps it was time to start taking life more seriously, and not treat work purely as a means to save for his adventurous pursuits.

The staff at the Records Office were very helpful and he had access to both newspapers and coroner's reports for the late eighteen-nineties.

He sat, quietly searching, in a room that had a musty smell of old documents, until a newspaper headline caught his eye. It was a piece in the *Southwest Courier* dated 15th July 1898.

It read:

Tragedy of young woman's suicide

Martha Bean, aged 21 from Penryn drowned herself by swimming out to sea until through exhaustion she slipped beneath the waves, the Coroner stated yesterday. Her body has not been found.

Her father, a widower and his two sons were lost at sea when their fishing ketch capsized in a gale, and it was thought that Miss Bean was overcome by grief. A witness, Susan Grant who was walking along the cliff top saw the young woman swim so far out that she disappeared from view.

A report on the coroner's proceedings gave the date of her suicide as the 5th June, and also included a photograph.

He stared at the date in disbelief; today was the 6th June, which meant it was the 5th yesterday when he had seen…. Well, what exactly had he seen, he now wondered and, strangest of all, the photo was the spitting image of the barmaid in the *Mariner's Arms*!

Nostalgia

W hen Albert Metcalf retired he began to daydream about his youth. In the garden on a summer's day, whilst cutting the grass, weeding the beds, dead-heading and doing all those little jobs one finds to do in the garden, he would suddenly pause, drop his tools and sit on the rustic bench. He would look up at a cotton-wool cloud and take flight, soaring skywards, until his detached suburban home in its executive-style estate shrank to the size of a matchbox and, even higher, a vista of green fields and ripe corn opened up as he travelled to the outskirts of another city; the city where he spent his childhood.

His wife, looking out of the window, smiled when she saw him, straw hat on head, dozing on the rustic seat.

In this dream-like state he descended from the azure sky to a row of little terrace houses, their front doors open to the cracked paving. The street was full of children, so many children, skipping, playing hopscotch and tag. There were no cars. A few ancient pushbikes leaned against hot brick walls. A woman, head wrapped in a scarf against the sun, knelt, black-shadowed, scrubbing her doorstep as though performing a religious rite.

At the far end he saw the milk cart turning the corner, pulled by Rosie, who didn't need telling where to stop because she knew that little Emily would run indoors and come rushing out with a carrot for her, whilst Lenny the milkman clattered two pints on her doorstep.

Outside the corner shop an enamelled sign had the inscription 'Players Please' beneath a picture of a bearded sailor. Albert knew that inside, amid the clutter of rainbow-sweet jars, twisted liquorice sticks, sherbet and bubble-gum, Tom would be collecting the ha'pennies from eager little hands.

Hovering above the street like some renaissance angel, he remembered going further afield to play and explore. The little terraces on the edge of town soon gave way to country lanes, and now his aerial flight took him a few miles on, to an overgrown area enclosed by trees, where sand had been excavated. Steep banks of crimson willow herb and ox-eye daisies led down to a shallow pool. The children loved this place; at weekends they spent hours building dens, playing cowboys, climbing mountains, fighting pirates, and being King of the Castle.

Albert sighed and opened his eyes. He had come to earth once more on his rustic seat. A light breeze caressed his face, a blackbird was singing in the apple tree.

"Martha," he said later that evening,

"I want to go back."

"Back? Back where to, dear?"

"To where I was brought up, to where I lived as a child; to see the old places."

"What brought this on?"

She smiled at the intensity of his expression.

"Nostalgia," he said.

"How will you get there?"

"By train."

"How long will you be?"

"A day should be enough. I might stay overnight somewhere."

Martha kissed him when she dropped him off at the train station.

"Things are never the same," she said as she drove off.

After arriving at the city centre Albert searched for, and eventually found, a bus going in the right direction. Half an hour later the driver called out, "Long Eaton! I thought someone was getting off here?"

Albert rose from his seat, confused; surely this couldn't be right? High-rise flats bordered the street.

"Long Eaton," confirmed the driver, "Renton Street stop."

He alighted and looked about him. The bus shelter was covered in a mad scribble of spray paint interspersed with obscenities. The terrace of his childhood was off Renton Street, but where was it? The bleakness of the concrete towers was enhanced by the concrete parking areas between them, upon which stood several burnt-out cars, like the blackened bones of extinct creatures from another time and place.

He quickened his pace until he came to a junction. The sign said Darwin Street. Yes, this is where he had lived, except that in those far off days it was called Darwin Terrace. The little houses had all gone, and in their place was a parade of shops.

A local convenience store with strong metal shutters guarding the front, a betting shop, a launderette, and a take-away from which emerged four youths laughing and horsing around. One was drinking from a can and, as they drew level he threw it on the ground. In a reflex action Albert picked it up and put it in a bin that was only a few feet away.

They all stopped in their tracks and the can-thrower glared at him.

"You trying to be funny?"

They all crowded around him. It was a tense moment, but they let him pass.

There was only one place now that he wanted to see, and that was the old sand quarry, where they had played as children.

The country lane was now an arterial road flanked by industrial units and a filling station. It was not exactly pedestrian-friendly, but he walked on a grass verge as the traffic thundered past.

He was just about to give up and retrace his steps, when he came to a fence and a notice that said 'Danger: Keep Out'. It was broken in several places and at one point there was a gap of about six feet, through which he entered. Facing him was a pile of builder's rubble that had been fly-tipped just inside the fence. This pyramid was topped with bags of rotting food waste and tin cans added by subsequent visitors.

Albert pushed his way through the fringe of trees and nettles, anxious to see the adventure playground of his youth. There were no flowers, just coarse grass sloping down to a stagnant, smelly pool. The edge, where yellow irises had once grown, now sprouted half-submerged shopping trolleys, discarded mattresses and baby buggies. Black engine oil was seeping into the ground from leaking, rusty tins. Albert had seen enough. By the time he had returned to Renton Street the sky had become overcast, washing the last vestiges of colour from this alien place that was his childhood home.

When Martha met him at the train station, the look on his face said it all. He did not have to speak.

"I told you so," she said, as she drove him home.

The next morning he woke early and, leaving his sleeping wife, he went into the garden. The sun shone from a cloudless sky. It must have rained in the night because it was damp underfoot and the air was fresh and sweet with blossom. He sat quietly on the rustic seat in the suburban garden of his detached house in its executive-style estate and listened to the morning sounds. The blackbird was singing joyously in his apple tree, and the early bees were buzzing in his borders. Was his childhood so idyllic? He had remembered the sun-filled happy days, but the hard, sad times had been relegated to the deep recesses of his subconscious. He sat quite still, ignoring the chill of a faint breeze, until he heard Martha clattering in the kitchen. A feeling of contentment permeated his being. The present was also a good time, a very good time.

Ambition

I t was one of those roads that run as straight as a die to the horizon, with scrubby vegetation on both sides as far as the eye can see. The only edifice in this god-forsaken landscape looked as if it had once been a farm building. It had a gas station forecourt with two pumps, and a rusting *Coca Cola* sign that swung gently on a metal stand.

From the forecourt an open door led into a room with a counter upon which was a coffee machine. Behind the counter were shelves, one containing confectionery and the other cigarettes. There was also a door that led off to the living quarters. The rest of the space in the room contained some tables and chairs.

Behind the counter, on a high stool, sat a woman smoking a cigarette; she looked about 70 but was, in fact, ten years younger.

Her son, who had recently celebrated his thirtieth birthday, was out on the forecourt cleaning his carefully restored Pontiac.

May Kitson and Marvin were the only ones in this isolated house, and they relied mainly on the passing trade of truck drivers to make a living. Marvin had often talked about expanding to meet the needs of these long-distance truckers, but they hadn't the cash or the energy to do anything about it.

He was cleaning his Pontiac because, it being a Saturday, he was going into Horseshoe Bend that evening, a small town some 25 miles away.

There wasn't much to do in Horseshoe Bend, unless you were a member of one of the three churches, which he was not. There were a number of bars, some of which were considered more respectable than others, and a hotel largely frequented by the town's shopkeepers and businessmen. But it was to one of the establishments with a more colourful reputation that Marvin was heading, because there he was more likely to score, and scoring with a girl was becoming something of an obsession with him.

His previous sexual experience was limited to a few furtive encounters, because it wasn't easy for an unmarried couple to have sex in Horseshoe Bend. For a start, there was nowhere you could take the girl, and most coupling was done on the back seat of an automobile. The trouble was that the Sheriff was a churchgoer and a puritan. His task, as he saw it, was to keep the community pure, and he had issued instructions to his officers to shine their torches into any vehicles parked in quiet spots, saying that he "wasn't going to allow no fornicating in his town." Marvin himself had been caught out in this way, much to both his and the girl's embarrassment.

On this particular night he wasn't having any luck either. He had started a conversation with the girl sitting at the bar next to him, when her boyfriend, who had been in the washroom, returned and glared at him.

Not wanting any trouble, he moved away and sat at a table with one of the other regulars.

He drove home in a state of intoxication but, luckily for him, he was not stopped by a patrol car.

There was not much trade on a Sunday and Marvin was slumped in a chair reading the comic section in the paper when he heard the sound of a horn honking incessantly.

"Impatient son of a bitch," May said. "Go and see what he wants."

There was nothing on the forecourt, the sound coming from the highway, so he walked along to the source, a stationary vehicle. Inside was a young woman.

"I have run out of gas," she said.

He bent his head to the open window.

"Release the brake, and I'll push you."

Back on the forecourt he looked at the old Chevy with disapproval. He opened the hood and a cloud of steam rose in the air. Marvin filled the radiator with water and told the girl to try and start the engine. It burst into life for a few minutes, emitting thick black smoke, and then died.

She opened the door and got out. Marvin looked at her appreciatively; she was wearing scruffy jeans and a shirt that showed a fair amount of cleavage, and had tousled, chestnut hair. He thought she was very pretty.

"Why don't you fill her up?" she said.

"No point; this pile of crap has had it. I dunno how far you've come, miss, but you sure as hell ain't going no further."

"I got to go further," she said, "I got to get to Las Vegas."

"I could drive you down town; you could stay at the *Bend Hotel*."

"I don't have much dough, and I've a job waiting in Vegas."

She turned and looked at the house.

"Can I stay here until I get my auto repaired?"

"It ain't worth repairin', and you don't have much dough."

She came closer to Marvin and smiled.

"You married?"

He shook his head.

"Girlfriend?"

"No."

"What's your name?"

"Marvin."

"Mine's Jane. Let me stay, Marvin, it won't be for long; I'm sure we can work something out."

Her eyelid flickered. Is she winking at me, he thought?

"I'll have to ask Ma."

"Ma?"

"Yes; I live here with her, and you'll have to sleep on a camp bed in the store room, because we don't have no place else."

May was none too pleased when he told her. He missed out the bit about the Chevy being fit for the scrap-yard.

"We ain't a hotel; just a few days then, and you'll have to pay."

"She don't have much," Marvin said, "she can serve customers for her keep."

May scowled at him.

"It don't take three of us."

He ignored this, and took Jane to see the storeroom.

"We'll fix this comfy for you," he said, kicking some boxes out of the way. Then they moved her Chevy off the forecourt and onto the back lot.

That night he lay in his bed thinking about the young woman who had arrived out of the dust in a clapped-out Chevy and was now sleeping under their roof. During the day he would stare at her, and she would stare back, breaking into a cheeky smile that said, "I know you fancy me, so when are you going to do something about it?"

He and his mother were looking out at Jane serving a customer on the forecourt. She was now wearing a short, denim skirt, and was in animated conversation with the driver.

"That floozy spells trouble; get rid of her quickly, take her to town and put her on a bus," May said.

"Trouble for who, Ma?"

"Both of us."

But Marvin had no intention of doing anything of the sort.

That evening he sat watching the Red Socks until after the other two had retired, and then he went to the storeroom.

"How you doing in here, Jane? Everythin' OK?"

Jane sat up in the bed, unconcerned that she had nothing on.

"I've slept in worse places."

He sat on the edge of the camp bed, making it creak and sag.

"Careful," she said, "This thing won't take both our weights."

He bent over her, his face a few inches from hers.

"My bed is much bigger than this."

"I thought you'd never ask," she said, getting up.

May must have heard noises coming from Marvin's room during the night, because she knocked at his door and called out, "Are you all right, son?"

Jane giggled, and Marvin said,

"Yeah, fine Ma."

In the morning Jane studied the smug expression on Marvin's face.

"Now don't you go getting any ideas about me hanging around, honey; I got ambitions, and this ain't part of it."

But after that night she no longer slept in the storeroom.

Then one evening she said,

"I got an idea; you can pay me to be a waitress."

May laughed out loud.

"What for? We don't do meals and, if we did, I wouldn't pay you."

"Listen, May, you cook fine for us, you were reared on a farm I guess; so why don't you get off your ass and cook for the truckers? They have plenty of dough."

"Did you hear that, Marvin? I'm not standing for it; if you like those guys so much, why don't you get one of them to give you a ride to wherever it is you wanna go? I'm sure you can repay them in kind."

"Calm down, Ma, think about it; we've talked about doing it before, so why not give it a try?"

May relented.

"Well, maybe I'll cook some plain fare, but we aren't paying her no wage," she said, looking at Jane. But by the end of the evening it was agreed that, instead of a wage, she would get a percentage of any profit they made on the meals.

It just so happened that the gas station was a convenient place for truck drivers to stop so, when steaks, French fries, eggs and all the other plain food were advertised, the café took off. Jane was a big hit, flirting with the men and showing even more cleavage as she leaned forward to put their meals in front of them. They started giving her tips, and this upset May, despite her benefiting from the increased income.

Marvin didn't mind her flirting; he wouldn't have minded what she did as long as she stayed with him, and he was beginning to think this was a possibility.

Then one day she said to him,

"The son of a bitch who sold me the Chevy screwed me good and proper and I don't intend for it to happen again, so would you take me into town and help me choose some wheels?"

"Wheels? Why, what you planning?"

"Jesus, Marvin, you know what I'm planning, I told you at the outset. I'm going to Vegas."

"What for? That job won't still be open for you."

"There is always a job for a girl with a good figure."

"Stay with me, Jane; Ma won't be around for ever, and between us we could do big things here and make some real dough."

"You must be kidding, honey; I got ambitions and this outfit don't figure in them. You're OK, Marvin; I like you, but I'm aimin' higher. You knew this was never meant to be permanent."

"OK, I'll take you first thing," he said with a sigh.

Next morning, they visited used-car showrooms in Horseshoe Bend. Marvin wanted to spin out this excursion as long as possible, so they looked at many vehicles before choosing the Buick he'd had his eye on from the start. They drove back to the lonely gas station, he following behind her, and he thought she could just put her foot down now and take off, and that would be it; but she returned to pick up her few possessions.

"Well, I guess it's time," she said, and kissed him, friendly like, on the cheek. Then she got into the Buick, gave him a wave and drove off.

He stood out in the highway watching the long, straight road until she disappeared in a faint cloud of dust.

When he returned, May was waiting for him.

"Well, we're back to normal now, son."

"Yeah, back to normal. You gonna continue with the meals?"

"Don't know, lot of work for two of us."

"Yeah, lot of work."

"Back to normal then, son."

An Old Man and a Tree

T he old man was stuck high up in the branches of a tree. He was sitting precariously on a branch, and holding on to a much smaller branch above his head. He was shivering uncontrollably, not so much with fright but with exertion, following the strenuous physical activity that resulted in his present predicament.

He had no idea how he was going to get down. It was one thing going up, but getting down was more difficult, especially as one of the branches had broken off with his weight, and only after much scrabbling and heaving had he had managed to gain his present perch. His muscles ached, but eventually the shivering stopped and his breathing became less laboured. The old man surveyed his surroundings. He could see the path winding through the wood and, in the distance, the tower of the parish church.

His eyes misted over, and below him a little girl about ten years old called out,

"Tommy, Tommy, can I come up too?"

"Girls can't climb trees."

"Yes I can," she said, struggling to reach the first branch.

To his surprise, Lucy soon appeared beside him.

"There, I told you I could."

"You've grazed your leg, and dirtied your frock," the boy said. "Your mum won't be pleased."

"I don't care," she said, "Can I be your best friend, Tommy?"

The memory left him. He was still up a tree and unable to get down, and he didn't care.

As a boy he had loved climbing trees. He had no fear of heights and would climb to the topmost branches, clinging to them as they bent and swayed under his weight.

They were destined for each other, Lucy and him. There had never been anyone else before he married her, even when he was doing National Service, and he'd had plenty of opportunities.

Afterwards he became a cartographer, and that gave him the opportunity to go to wild places, and so he graduated from tree-climbing to mountaineering. In the early days of their marriage Lucy accompanied him on these expeditions, but first her own career, and then the birth of a son put an end to this.

Her attitude to mountains was different from his. He remembered a time when they were climbing in a remote part of the Caucasus. It had been difficult terrain and, although very tired, they were not far from the summit. He had wanted to press on, but Lucy said she was turning back. For her, reaching the summit was not important; the physical exertion, the clear mountain air, and the sight of a soaring eagle were enough. For him, the summit was a goal that had to be achieved. Not getting there amounted to failure, but he could not let her descend on her own, it was too dangerous, so he was resentful. Why couldn't she make that extra effort? They could have made it in under an hour. By the time they had made camp he had calmed down; he was still disappointed, but there would be other mountains, and other climbing holidays.

Then, after their son was born the holidays became less strenuous, more relaxed, but good fun nevertheless. Cumbria was a favourite place. There was still physical activity, of course; rowing on a lake, climbing the hills, and going on walks, but it was more leisurely, and happy family memories of this time brought sweet, sentimental tears to his eyes.

Then there was the time when they were both absorbed in their work, preoccupied with advancing their careers, and here his face clouded over as he recalled meeting Stella at a conference. They had an affair that lasted six months. They were good friends, but not in love; it was all about the sex. Lucy never found out, but it was only now, in the tree, that feelings of guilt at this betrayal overwhelmed him.

Their son, Casper, met and married an Australian girl, and decided to emigrate. He and Lucy had been out to Perth several times to see their grandchildren. Casper had been back with the family once as, with three children, it was an expensive business to make the journey home.

Then Lucy started having health problems. She experienced strange weaknesses in her limbs, and other odd symptoms. After being referred to one hospital specialist, who referred her on to a consultant at another, she was eventually diagnosed as having a rare neurological condition for which there was no cure. They were both shocked to learn that the disease was progressive, and would end in her death.

They kept the bad news from their son and, as Lucy deteriorated, Tom took early retirement to look after his wife. He bought a van and had it converted to accommodate Lucy. It had an electric tail-lift, making it easy for her to access the vehicle in her wheelchair.

A downstairs bedroom was created, with everything to hand for the care staff now coming in to the house several times daily, as Lucy needed more help than he alone could give her. One day, when Lucy's doctor called, he took Tom aside and asked if he had considered the possibility of Lucy being cared for in a nursing home. Tom said he wouldn't hear of it and, anyway, it was not what she wanted.

His only break from the daily routine occurred when a rota of volunteers sat with her for a few hours several times each week and, on these occasions, he would often walk through the wood on the far side of the village. It contained some fine old oaks, but there was one specimen that he always stopped to admire, and imagined climbing. In his head he worked out the exact sequence of steps necessary, where to put his feet, which branches to grip, and which part would be the most difficult. He decided the main problem was the distance the first branch was from the ground. In his youth this would not have been an issue; he could have easily swung himself up with the agility of a gymnast, but now it was a different story.

It was sad to see Lucy, who had always been so self-assured and independent, having to rely on others for all her daily needs. She was becoming completely helpless, and she began to lose the power of speech.

Tom was very tired now, and his arms ached as he clung to the branch above him. He remembered the day that, with the aid of the electronic gadgetry she now used, she told him she'd had enough and she wanted him to assist her to end her life. At first he had resisted, but how could he assess the degree of pain she was experiencing? All he knew was that he hated to see her suffer, and what mattered was that she had no quality of life, and for her this was intolerable. But he had prevaricated, and waited too long, so that it was no longer a question of assisting her. He would have to do the deed.

He had not walked along the path through the wood for several days and, since the last time, some men had been at work felling a dead tree next to his favourite oak, the one he imagined himself climbing. The branches had been sawn up, and converted into neat piles of logs, and the main trunk into sections of about a metre in length. One of these heavy sections had fallen at the base of the oak, and Tom stood looking at it for some time. He glanced around, but there was no one to be seen this weekday morning, so he stood on the trunk and reached up.

Was it really just two hours ago they had said their farewells? They were not believers; there was no afterlife, so they bid each other a tender goodbye. Lucy's carers, who had a key, would have let themselves in by now, and called the police.

Fatigue overwhelmed the old man, and his muscles cramped in pain. He relaxed his grip on the branch above him and swayed gently on his perch. He thought of all the good times he and Lucy had had together and brought his hands down to his sides. Pitching forwards, he caught a glimpse of green leaves and dappled sunlight as he crashed headlong through the sturdy branches.

An Unlikely Friendship

W ally, the solicitor's clerk, looked up from his desk where he had been reading the headlines in the *Evening Standard* and announced to the room in general,

"Gawd knows what will happen now that Atlee's got in; that's all the thanks Winnie gets for saving the country."

He looked at the two legal secretaries, who just tittered and got on with their typing, so he reluctantly turned to the office-boy, Jack, who was sticking stamps on letters.

"Oh, I don't know, Labour have got some good ideas; they don't just help the toffs."

"I didn't ask for your stupid opinion, boy."

Jack disliked Wally, who'd been at the firm of Rankin, Ford and Chester all his working life and was embittered by this fact.

Wally looked at his watch.

"Better get a move on, lad, if you're going to catch the post."

Jack walked down the rickety stairs of the bomb-damaged Georgian terrace. The legal enclave of Gray's Inn had suffered from the Luftwaffe, and there were gaping holes in the sedate facades. In High

Holborn he was passing the blind concertina-player who stood on the corner of Chancery Lane, when the mailbag slipped from his shoulder onto the pavement.

"Careful, boy! You break anything and you'll be in hot water for sure."

"There's nothing breakable; anyway, how did you know I was young? I thought you were supposed to be blind?"

"I have ears! I heard you say a rude word; and I'm not completely blind, I see shadows. I know what's going on round here - you'd be surprised."

Jack laughed.

"See the couple in the doorway to your right? They work in Clifford's Inn, and they are having an affair. He's married."

"If you say so, Mr Holmes!"

The next day, in his lunch hour, Jack stopped by the concertina player.

"Hello."

"It's the boy who drops things, isn't it?"

"You don't have much in your cap. I don't have any money, but you can share my sandwiches if you like.

"They are only jam, but my landlady says I am lucky to get that, what with the rationing. What's your name?"

"They call me Len, Canadian Len, on account of the fact that I spent a lot of my life in Canada."

"My name's Jack."

"OK boy."

They walked to Lincoln's Inn Fields, Len white stick in hand and still wearing his concertina, suspended by a strap. Jack decided he could see far better than he let on.

"I'll tell you a secret," Len said, when they sat down.

"You never leave more than a few pennies in the hat. That way people feel sorry for you, and they drop their change in, even if they don't like your music."

"Where did you learn to play?"

"Nowhere. Taught myself, but I only know six tunes!"

Jack shared out the sandwiches.

"You are a bit young to have a landlady; where's your parents?"

"Don't know. Haven't got any, I'm a Barnardo's boy. When I started work they placed me with Mr and Mrs Pegler. I get thirty shillings a week, and have to pay twenty-five shillings for my keep. Mrs Pegler gives me breakfast, a sandwich lunch, and dinner in the evening."

"You've got it made, son."

"I don't think so. I've got no certificates, and my future is uncertain. I don't want to stay at the solicitors and become a crotchety old bloke like Wally."

"You'll be OK, boy, you will make something of yourself, I can tell. Not be a waster like me."

"I thought you served in the Great War?"

"I did, lad, but not in Flanders; I was a merchant seaman. I saw some action, and spent some time in an open boat before being picked up."

"Your family must have been pleased you were saved."

"Family? What family? You and me are in the same boat; I got no family. I was brought up by some religious order whose monks beat the hell out of me. I never settled in a job, or stayed with a woman for long, and I was too fond of the booze. Don't touch a drop now, though."

"Where do you live, Len?"

"A Salvation Army hostel in Whitechapel. You can't keep anything there because it gets nicked, but seeing as how I've been there a while, the Major allows me to keep a few things in a locked cupboard."

They met up in Jack's lunch hour for the rest of that week, and he asked Mrs Pegler for more sandwiches.

"Do you think I'm made of money? What you give me doesn't run to it. I give you a proper dinner, don't I?"

Jack missed his chats with the concertina player over the weekend so, on the Monday, he was looking forward to their meeting, but when he arrived at the corner of Chancery Lane Len wasn't there. He went into the tobacconist's shop next to his pitch and asked,

"Where's Len?"

"Len?"

"The blind concertina-player."

"Oh, him. I don't know; he was here on Saturday."

Jack wondered what had happened to his friend so when, on the next day, he was given some documents needing urgent delivery to a firm in the City, he decided to make some enquiries. From the top deck of the bus he could see the havoc caused by the blitz, the blackened dome of St Paul's standing out like a ship in a sea of destruction. This dismal scene was lightened by the red of the willow herb on the bombsites, and the buddleia growing in tortured shapes from the crumbling brickwork.

After delivering his documents he headed further east. Wally would be mad at him for being late back, but he did not care. The Salvation Army Major was sympathetic.

"Canadian Len, laddie, you know him? I'm sorry to tell you that he had a heart attack on Sunday. He was unconscious when they took him to the London Hospital. I'm sorry I can't be of any more help, but homeless men come and go in this place, and we never enquire about their background."

Jack walked the short distance to the hospital. At reception he spoke to the head porter.

"A man named Len was admitted as an emergency on Sunday. He had a heart attack. I'd like to see him."

"Oh you would, would you? Has this Len got a surname?"

"I don't know what it is."

"I see; so you are not a relative?"

"No."

"What's he to you, then? Don't answer that, I'd rather not know; but I do know he's none of your business, so clear off, young man. And if you come back, I'll call the police."

A young nurse, who'd been standing nearby and overheard the conversation, caught up with Jack in the street.

"There was no need for him to treat you like that. I think I know whom you mean. Were you his friend?"

"Yes."

"If he was the one who came from a hostel, I'm afraid he died."

"What will happen to him?"

"As there are no relatives to claim the body, no doubt the medical students will practise on him."

"And then?"

"He'll be buried in an unmarked grave somewhere; sorry, I can't say where, or when."

Jack called back at the hostel to let the Major know Len was dead.

"What will you do with his things?"

The Major sighed and produced a bag of old clothes, the battered-looking concertina, and an envelope with ten shillings and sixpence inside.

"This is all he owned."

"Can I have the squeeze-box?"

"I don't know, lad."

"To remember him by."

"Well, it is in a bit of a state, and probably not worth much. I'm breaking regulations but… all right then."

Back at Gray's Inn, Jack hid the concertina in the cloakroom and prepared himself for Wally's wrath.

That night, as Jack was lying awake, Len appeared at the foot of his bed and started playing the familiar tunes.

"Shush, you will wake the Peglers," Jack said.

It was a dream, of course, although he could have sworn he put the concertina on top of the chest of drawers; but, in the morning, as the sun shone through the gap in the curtains, it was on the chair by the window.

Kinky Susan

She was known around Soho as Kinky Susan, on account of the way she dressed. Sometimes in leather with fishnet stockings and high heels, sometimes with chains around her neck and thigh boots, sometimes in a nun's outfit, but with a very short skirt. The people she met never knew what she was going to wear next. You wouldn't have thought that Susan was a shy person, but she had that ability, possessed by many actors, of changing their personality when they were acting a role and, when she ventured out she was projecting an image of the kind of person she felt she was at heart.

The truth was her life experiences had made her feel insecure, but somewhere in her psyche there was a theatrical fantasy-figure trying to get out. Striding through Soho streets, ignoring tourists, breathing the spicy air rich with fragrance wafting from many restaurants, she made her way to the *Zambezi*, the club where she worked until the early hours. Although not conventionally attractive, her face was plain and her nose rather too large, she did have a sensuous figure and was sufficiently intriguing for customers to buy her drinks, and frequently proposition her.

Susan turned them down because she wasn't promiscuous, and anyway, she did not trust these men who just wanted casual sex. She wasn't sure what she wanted, but she knew it wasn't a succession of one-night stands. Karl, the owner of the club, was quite happy with her presence as she was good for business, and so her life became a routine of sleeping, often until midday or later, having lunch, sometimes at a café down the street if she had forgotten to buy any food, doing chores and listening to records or the radio until it was time for dinner. Then she would rummage through her wardrobe, deciding what of her outfits she would wear that evening.

The club did not begin to get busy until after eleven, but Susan would arrive early to tidy the place and turn on the fan in an effort to disperse the smell of stale smoke that permeated the basement room. Then she would empty ashtrays and wash up any glasses left from the previous night. The decor was Art Nouveau, with racy Aubrey Beardsley prints on the walls. Some customers were regulars whom Susan and Karl knew by name, artists and Soho characters with dubious occupations; others were businessmen who came from time to time. Then there were the casuals; you had to be a member, but it was easy to become one. If Fred, the doorman, liked the look of you he simply gave you a form to fill in.

It was early and only a few regulars were sipping their drinks, one trying to read the evening paper in the dim light, when a new member came in. He stared at Susan, who was wearing her nun's costume, and seemed lost for words.

"What can I get you to drink?" she said.

"I'll have a large whisky with a little water," the stranger said, sitting down.

Susan brought the whisky to his table with a small jug of water, and he was transfixed by the incongruity of a nun with a short skirt. He followed her with his eyes as she returned to the bar and busied herself behind the counter. It was still very quiet, and so Karl went over to the newcomer's table."Come very far?"

"No," he said laconically, still looking at Susan.

It was one of Karl's good days and he felt in an expansive mood.

"If you are thinking what I think you are, you're wasting your time with Susan, she doesn't...." He stopped, not wanting to be too crude with a new customer.

"I'd like her to model for me."

"You a photographer?"

"No, I paint portraits."

"You'd better buy her a drink, then, and ask her."

He introduced himself as Simon, and asked if she would sit for him.

She studied his face. Inquisitive blue eyes, a small beard neatly trimmed, and shoulder-length hair.

"So you are an artist."

It was a statement, and he didn't reply.

"How much are you paying?"

"I'm not paying anything, but I want you to sit for me; you have very interesting features."

"What do I get out of it?"

"I'll give you some lunch."

She laughed derisively.

"Where's your studio?"

"Spitalfields."

"You want my clothes off?"

"Yes and no. No, because I want to paint you in what you are wearing now."

"And yes because?" She raised an eyebrow.

"You have a sensuous figure."

"Well you can forget any ideas you may have about that, and," she added, "you can refund my fare."

His attic studio was a jumble of oil paints, brushes, white canvases, framed and unframed paintings, and discarded detritus on the floor. At one end there was a raised wooden platform upon which stood a chair.

"Just sit in the chair," he said, "with your hands on your lap."

He stared at her for some time before turning to his easel.

She stared back and then broke into a sly smile.

"Can I talk?"

"Yes, if you have anything to say."

"This place smells, and it needs a good clean."

"It's the way I like it."

"Where do you live?"

"Downstairs."

"Do I have to keep still?"

"Within reason; don't decide to pick your nose."

She laughed, and he noted that her rather sad face lit up.

They were both silent for a while, he concentrating, she getting bored; then she crossed her legs, making the short skirt of her nun's outfit ride even higher.

"Can you uncross your legs?"

"Why? Does it make any difference?"

"It's not the way I want it."

Rebuked, she was silent for the rest of the session.

Later, she wondered why she had agreed to sit for this man but, even as the thought struck her, she knew the answer; she was attracted to him.

Sitting for Simon became part of her routine. They had their lunches together, and she felt comfortable with him, but she had not been allowed to see the painting, until one day when she arrived the chair had gone and he told her the painting was finished.

When he showed her she was transfixed. She concentrated her gaze on the face, because in her face he had captured the inner sadness, her insecurity, the very depths of her psyche.

"I fear you know me too well," was all she said.

There was a low divan where the chair had been and, without any word from him, she went behind the corner screen and undressed. She then lay on the divan and asked if that was how he wanted her.

At the end of the session she rose and went to go behind the screen, but he caught her in his arms. She did not resist.

Susan was falling in love, but she knew that this affair would not end well, and she tried to rein in her emotions.

The second painting was eventually finished, but this time Simon did not let her see it. He thanked her and kissed her; it was a goodbye kiss and she had no doubt that he already had a new model sitting for him.

The routine of her life returned to the time before she met Simon, but she was less flirtatious with customers than previously, and Karl noticed the sad smile when they tried to chat her up.

Then one day he said,

"Your artist friend is exhibiting at the Royal Academy Summer Exhibition; his paintings have caused quite a stir."

"How do you know?"

"I read the reviews."

She rose earlier than usual the next morning and, putting on the most inconspicuous clothes she could find, with some trepidation paid a visit to the exhibition.

She wandered through the gallery until she came to a group of people standing in front of two paintings.

At first she could not see, but then someone moved aside and, as she had already suspected, they were of her.

In a reference to Goya's famous paintings, supposedly of the Duchess of Alba, they were titled *Susan Clothed*, and *Susan Unclothed*. Although she was familiar with the first one she hardly dared to look at it, so much did the face reflect what she had been feeling. The second painting was entirely different. She had been lying on her side in a way that emphasised the curve of her hip running down to the hollow of her waist and, with an arm under her breasts it was intended to be erotic.

It was the face that upset her though, because it so reflected the change in her feelings. It looked out at the artist with undisguised love. There could be no doubt that the artist and his model were lovers.

She stared at the painting for some time, and then she noticed a young man was looking from her to the paintings, and then back to her. He was about to say something, but she quickly moved away and, with a sigh, walked briskly out of the courtyard and down Piccadilly.

The Quality of Mercy

Rosa Kaduna was just fifteen; it had been her birthday the previous week. She lived with her mother in a shack on the edge of town – one of a group of rickety, thrown-together abodes sharing one water-tap.

Mugabe and his henchmen had called them parasites, illegal squatters, and they lived in fear of being forcibly removed.

Rosa was walking along the dusty road when it happened. She saw trouble approaching; a group of young men, drinking, shouting, laughing, fuelled on alcohol, cavorting all over the road. She slowed her pace, wondering what she should do. They immediately noted her hesitation and called out to her obscenely. Rosa turned and retraced her steps, and the young men followed with quickened pace. She was scared, and began to run. In response, they also broke into a run. They soon caught up with her and dragged her off the road into the bushes, where she was raped by four of the young men. Her violation was ugly, and without pity. They left her in shock, dishevelled, dirty and traumatised.

When she arrived home Martha, her mother, held her close and tried to sooth the floods of tears.

"We must go to the police station," she said.

They walked the two miles to the police station in the centre of town, and Rosa told the sergeant on duty what had happened to her.

He looked at her without compassion.

"I can't get a doctor to come here today," he said, and yawned.

"You will have to come back tomorrow. In the meantime, please do not wash yourself."

She wanted to scrub herself from head to toe, but she nodded blankly.

The next day, Rosa and her mother walked back to the police station, where a doctor examined her.

"She needs medication," he said to Martha. "Have you money? I can get the drugs, but it will be expensive."

He knew the answer before Martha shook her head.

"Then I can't help you," he said, closing his bag.

Had Joshua, her husband, still been alive, and working, they would have found the money somehow. When Rosa was little they had lived in Harare, where he was a civil servant, but he had joined the Movement for Democratic Change, critical of Robert Mugabe's human rights record and, as a consequence, had been sacked from his post. Not long afterwards he was trampled to death at a party rally when it was charged by baton-wielding police. After that, things went from bad to worse for Martha and her daughter, and now they were struggling to survive.

As they walked home, Martha considered what she should do.

Joshua had a brother in Harare called Thomas. He was a shady character, a bit of a black sheep, and so there had been little contact between them when he was alive. Martha now resolved to go to Harare and seek him out.

They packed a few things in a bag and went out on to the highway. Eventually, a truck driver picked them up and took them to the city.

They went to her brother-in-law's old neighbourhood, and were soon directed to his house.

He heard their story in silence.

"There's not much I can do, Martha, but you can stay here for a few days. Joshua was a political activist, so the best thing you can do is to claim asylum in the UK. Why don't you go to the British High Commission, and see what they say? If they can help, I'll pay your fares."

At the High Commission they waited a long time, but were eventually seen by an official. Martha explained that her husband had been killed whilst taking part in a peaceful anti-government demonstration, and that her daughter had been raped, and that they wanted to go to Britain.

"What would be the purpose of your visit?" he said.

"Asylum," she said naively, "to seek asylum."

"That is not grounds for a visa application," he said for the fourth time that morning, "and there is no legal way you can travel to the UK without one."

He looked at mother and daughter critically.

"If you can produce bank statements to show that you have adequate funds to support yourselves, and you know someone in the UK who will sponsor and vouch for you, and if you also undertake not to use the National Health Service during your stay other than as a private patient, we might give you a two-months' visa."

He stood up; the interview was at an end.

Martha's brother-in-law showed no surprise when she told him the outcome, and he had more bad news for her. He'd heard that Mugabe's men had flattened the squatter's settlement where they lived and the people had been taken in trucks and just dumped somewhere in the bush.

They no longer had a home to go to.

Martha shed some tears, and Thomas paced up and down the room a few times.

"There is one thing I can do," he said; "it will cost me, and I don't know why I should go to all this expense for my brother's wife, when he looked down on me when he was alive, but I'll get you some forged papers. After that you are both on your own."

It took longer to obtain the documents than he anticipated, and Thomas sighed with relief as he saw them off at the airport. At the barrier their papers were scrutinised and, for a heart-stopping moment, Martha thought they would not be allowed to board the aircraft, but the officer nodded and returned the documents to them.

It was a different story at Heathrow, however. They were soon singled out and called to one side by an immigration officer, who left them in an interviewing room whilst he went off with their documents. He returned with a senior colleague, who threw the documents down on the table.

"All these are forged," he said, "including this South African passport. What have you to say?"

"I want to claim asylum here for myself and my daughter," she replied.

"Never mind about asylum," the officer said, "you have committed a serious offence, and we could put you on the next flight back to Harare."

"I want to claim asylum," Martha repeated.

"I have to tell you," the other officer said, "that forged documents are considered reason enough for refusing asylum."

Martha did not reply. The officer looked at Rosa, who had started sobbing.

"Have you anyone here, a responsible citizen in regular employment, who would stand surety for you?" he asked, softening his tone slightly.

She shook her head.

"Then I'm afraid we must detain you both."

It was very late when Martha and her daughter arrived at the Immigration Removal Centre, a prison-like establishment run by the private sector and, as they fell into a troubled sleep, they wondered what the future would hold.

They discovered the inmates were of many nationalities; some had already had their claims rejected and were awaiting deportation, or the outcome of an appeal, whilst others had served a prison sentence and were being held until they could be sent back to their country of origin. There were even some unaccompanied children under eighteen whose parents had been killed by some militia group or other. A lady from a voluntary organisation visited them and she put them in touch with a lawyer, who paid them several visits. He told them that the government was tightening up on bogus asylum-seekers, due to public pressure and campaigns in the tabloid press and, as a result, their case was to be fast-tracked. Also, the government had capped legal fees, and so he could not devote as much time to their case as he would have liked.

A few weeks passed by, and Rosa became ill. The doctor was not happy with her symptoms and arranged for her to attend the local hospital. Martha insisted on going with her, and so she was accompanied by one of the security staff in case she decided to abscond. Martha told the doctor that her daughter had been raped. They kept Rosa in for some tests and, when Martha was next taken to visit, she was told that her daughter was HIV positive, and they would be prescribing anti-retroviral drugs.

Time passed, and mother and daughter waited anxiously for the outcome of their claim for asylum. Then the lawyer visited them again. He had some bad news; their claim had been rejected. He showed them the papers. Notwithstanding the fact that her husband had been an active member of the opposition party, it said, there was no evidence that as a result of his activities Mrs Kaduna and her daughter were being persecuted, or that their lives were in danger from the regime, and so the application was rejected.

The lawyer put his hand on Martha's shoulder.

"I'm so sorry," he said; "we can appeal, we must appeal," but his voice betrayed his lack of conviction regarding the outcome.

"We cannot go back to Zimbabwe," Martha said, "there is nothing for us there; we will be destitute and without drugs Rosa will die."

"I will do my best," was all he could say.

They had no alternative except to hope that the decision would be reversed on compassionate grounds but, in the end, their appeal was rejected. The final straw came after that. They were informed that, as they were now awaiting deportation, they could not receive free treatment from the National Health Service unless it was in an emergency and, consequently, Rosa would no longer receive the expensive anti-retroviral drugs that she was currently prescribed.

Martha became hysterical and told staff that they had no future, and there was no point in them going on living. They both threatened they would kill themselves if asylum was not reconsidered, but deportation day grew nearer without any change of heart by the authorities.

It was a member of staff who found them both, early one morning, hanging in the toilets, and the tragedy was reported widely in the media.

Radio's *Today* programme asked if a minister would come on to discuss the issues, but none was available. Instead, the Department issued a statement.

"This is a very sad case," it said, "but there are strict rules governing asylum, and we cannot give in to emotional blackmail."

Oh Mr Stanislavsky!

The childless couple lived in a fashionable apartment in the centre of a northern city. The husband, Elliot, was a banker and his wife, Anne, a part-time salesperson in a department store. She didn't have to work, but she needed something to occupy her time, and she liked her job. Her passion, though, was amateur dramatics, and the few friends that she had made since moving to the city were members of her group.

She had wanted a child, but it had not happened in six years and, as Elliot appeared content, she had not broached the possibility of them seeking medical advice.

They had been passionate lovers during the first few years of their marriage, but now he worked long hours and returned home exhausted. He would even fall asleep while she was telling him about her day. Stopping in mid-sentence, she reflected that much of the romance had gone from their relationship, which deteriorated into a comfortable routine.

Anne had got herself co-opted onto the committee of the *20ᵗʰ Century Players*, an old, established amateur dramatic company whose productions alternated between popular shows and more serious, even experimental, contemporary drama.

Tanya directed the plays and musicals that were their bread and butter, and Leon the less commercial productions. He fancied himself as a director, and had absorbed influences as diverse as Lee Strasberg, Joan Littlewood and Mike Leigh. A committee meeting had been called to discuss a play by a hitherto unknown playwright who had sent in a script. Leon had been very impressed, and had circulated copies.

"We should give new talent a chance," Leon said.

"In my opinion, this young playwright has a future, and it would be great if we were the ones to discover him."

After a lengthy discussion they agreed to stage *Unreal City*, as the play was called. One of the most important characters in the play was a prostitute, and Leon wanted Anne to play this role.

Anne was flattered, but had to be convinced that she was right for the part. Elliot seemed preoccupied with bank matters, so she did not get around to telling him her news.

Rehearsals got under way, and Leon suggested that she broaden the hint of a Lancashire accent that she already possessed, and give it an earthier, common edge.

One evening, Leon took Anne aside and said that next time she should dress the part.

"But we aren't ready for a dress rehearsal yet; why me?"

"Because your role is pivotal and I want you to immerse yourself in the character."

On the morning of the next rehearsal, Elliot announced that he was going to London on bank business and wouldn't be returning until the following day.

She arrived at the hall early in order to prepare herself. With help, she found the clothes she was looking for and emerged somewhat self-consciously from the dressing room in a very short skirt, bare legs with high-heeled sandals, a skimpy top, a short, white leather jacket and a blonde wig.

"Excellent," Leon said after the rehearsal, but what really pleased her was the compliment paid by David Field, the playwright who, in discussion with the cast, had been making some changes to the script. She had been about to get changed when Leon said,

"Why don't you stay in the role you are playing a bit longer? Go home dressed as you are; it will help you identify with the character. You can pick up your clothes tomorrow."

Anne hesitated, because she thought she already identified with the character, but Leon persisted, and she gave in. On the bus the only seats vacant were near the front and facing each other and, when she sat down, her skirt rode up higher than she would have liked. She kept her legs together and self-consciously tugged at the hem, as a man opposite stared at her. Why, she thought, was it that she was not disturbed about exposing her legs in the theatre? The answer was obvious - because she was acting a role; and that was what she had to do now.

She alighted from the bus at the next stop, some distance from her apartment, and started teetering carefully down the street in her high heels. She was very near the red light area of the city, and found herself being drawn towards it. How she would react if she were propositioned she was not sure, but she certainly would not have gone off with a stranger. There were not many girls about this particular evening, and those that were were not friendly. She was a newcomer, or so they thought, poaching on their territory, and she scurried away as they shouted abuse.

Enough of this role-playing, she thought, I want to go home, but she had just reached the corner of the street when a car cruised up slowly and stopped beside her. She was about to walk on quickly when she hesitated, because the car seemed familiar. The person inside wound down the window, and she realised with a shock that it was Elliot.

He did not recognise her in her blonde wig. She clenched her fists in anger and disbelief, and then she decided to act the part. She put her face close to the open window and said,

"Hello love, you looking for business?"

Elliot recognised the voice and puzzlement gave way to incredulity as she pulled off her wig.

"What the fuck are you doing?" he said.

"I could ask you the same thing."

"For Christ's sake, get in the car."

She got in beside him and slammed the door.

"I thought you were in London."

"I was, but we finished early, and I drove back."

"But not home. What were you doing trying to pick up a prostitute, and where did you intend taking her?"

He looked shamefaced for a moment, and then became angry.

"More to the point, what the hell were you doing trying to pick up men? Is this what you do when I think you are at rehearsals?"

"Don't be stupid; I was acting a role. Our director is keen on a school of acting known as The Method, originated by a man called Stanislavsky, and he wanted me to spend some time wearing the clothes of the character I am playing; but I had no intention of going off with anyone. In fact, when you pulled up my first instinct was to run. Now I'm waiting for your explanation!"

"I, that is we, finished our business early," he stammered.

"You told me that."

"Well, I knew you would be out, and I didn't want to go home, so I booked into a hotel. After all, you weren't expecting me."

He looked out of the window.

"I had better not stay here any longer," he said and, putting the car into gear he drove off.

"Cut the crap, Elliot; why were you trying to pick up a prostitute?"

"I don't know; things haven't been all that good between us lately, have they? I mean, when I think what we were like a few years ago?"

"So that's your excuse. Well that's very funny, because I've been getting the distinct impression that you have lost interest in me. Do you think dozing in front of the telly is going to get me aroused?"

Elliot stole a sideways glance at his wife, taking in her expanse of thigh.

"Have I ever told you that you have very nice legs?"

"Don't schmooze me, Elliot; I'm still angry; and where are we going? This isn't the way home."

"To the *Royal Northern*, of course; I have paid for one of their best rooms, so we may as well use it."

"I see; so you want me to go in with you dressed like this, so everyone will think you have picked me up. What do you take me for?"

"Well I did pick you up, didn't I? Anyway, I thought you were practising being in character, so now is your chance to act the role."

She glared at him, and was silent for the rest of the journey. At the hotel she decided to hang on to Elliot's arm as she clip-clopped across the foyer, just because she didn't hink a prostitute would do that; but, as they passed reception, she could swear the man behind the counter winked at Elliot.

As soon as they were in the room he opened the minibar and poured himself a gin and tonic.

"Are you having one?" he asked, sitting in one of the two easy chairs.

Anne looked at the king-size bed.

"If you are staying here, you can get me a taxi."

Elliot got up and faced her.

"Don't go. What can I say except I'm very sorry? I have no excuse; I have been working hard, you have your own interests and I thought we were drifting apart. We weren't communicating."

He put his arms around her.

"And whose fault is that?" Anne said.

"You know you look very sexy in that outfit."

"If I'm staying here, that will be a hundred pounds, cash," she replied.

"Don't be bloody silly."

"I'm serious; you were going to pay for it, and I don't suppose the girl you picked up would have accepted credit cards. Anyway, I'm acting a role, remember!"

"Have it your way then," he said, walking her backwards towards the bed.

After the rehearsal the following week, Leon asked Anne how she had got on carrying out his experiment of staying 'in role.'

"Very illuminating," she said, "I went to the red light district and picked up a man."

He looked at her in astonishment.

"You're joking! I don't believe you; that is going too far - you wouldn't."

Anne put on her coat and slung her bag over her shoulder.

"I'm serious," she said, heading for the door, "but don't worry; the man I picked up turned out to be my husband!"

A Strange Portrait

O n cold winter mornings I am in the habit of visiting art galleries. The temperature is usually just right, and the lighting subdued to protect the paintings, and so the atmosphere is like visiting a stately home in the off-season. When your feet begin to ache there is usually a bench to sit on and, if you are early enough, you may be the only one quietly meditating in front of some picture. In national collections and municipal galleries you will have the company of a bored guard yawning beside the entrance who, in many cases, will not say a single word to you unless you have the temerity to ask him a question.

On this day I found myself staring at the picture of a beautiful woman, richly attired in 16th-century finery. I looked at the little card by the side; the title was *Isabella D'Adamo* and, underneath, the name of the artist, who was unfamiliar to me, although I pride myself on being acquainted with most of the renaissance painters. Such was the intense realism of this masterpiece that it could have been the work of Caravaggio.

I rested on a conveniently-placed bench and examined the painting more closely. To judge by her dress and the background furnishings she was a woman of means, and she sat prettily in her silken gown, her long, chestnut hair draped artfully around her shoulders. I was mesmerised by her face, a face that expressed a deep sadness, reflected in the eyes that looked directly at the unknown artist who painted her.

Was she grieving, I wondered? What tragedy had befallen her all those years ago? Perhaps she had lost someone near and dear to her. If only I could research the mystery. I gazed and gazed at the painting and found myself increasingly drawn towards it. I stood up and looked around me. The only other person, the guard, was dozing, and so I went up to the picture and, to my great surprise, I found I was able to walk right in.

I found myself standing in her richly-furnished saloon, and I moved well to one side so as not to obstruct the view of the artist; but I need not have worried, because it was clear that neither of them could see me.

The first thing I noticed was the odour; it was unpleasant and overpowering, and it appeared to be emanating from the lady. She had tried to mask it with various fragrances but, in truth, this just added to the assault on the senses. I then noticed that the artist had a kerchief around his face, covering his nose. Suddenly he moved forward to study his subject more closely, and then he moved back again with alacrity. I now understood the lady's problem; despite her beauty she was isolated by her own body odour, an odour she could not control.

I should say at this point that I have a fair knowledge of Italian, gained from my younger days when I spent some time studying in Rome, so that when the artist spoke I understood every word.

"Signorina, it is enough. I have done all I can; come look at your portrait."

The artist withdrew a safe distance from Isabella as, her eyes lighting up with excitement, she peered at the other side of the easel for the first time.

"Wonderful," she said, "I am very pleased; it is an excellent likeness, but it goes beyond that; it's as though you can read my thoughts. Thank you, Giovanni."

I was surprised by her familiarity but, when I looked at the artist with his face uncovered, it was apparent that he was a handsome young man, and Isabella would have liked to be more intimate with him than her affliction permitted.

He smiled and said, "I have a good friend, a fine craftsman, who will frame your picture for you."

He called for his assistant to help carry his equipment, and took his leave without venturing too close to Isabella. She gave some deep sighs as soon as she was alone but, tempted as I was to stay, I quickly caught up with Giovanni and followed him all the way to his studio. I had not been there very long when the artist's picture-framer friend turned up, and Giovanni opened a bottle of wine. He swirled and sniffed his glass.

"This is a great vintage, Angelo; pity you can't smell the fruits."

"That may be so, but I can taste and, more to the point, I can feel the effect."

They talked as they drank and, let me tell you, there is nothing worse than watching two men getting tipsy when you can't join in and have a drink yourself. Then my ears pricked up as Giovanni said,

"I have a commission for you. I have just finished painting the most beautiful woman, and I want you to frame the portrait. You should see her, Angelo; I could lose my heart to her, were it not for...how can I put this delicately? She has an affliction that no amount of bathing alleviates. To put it more bluntly, her body smells most foul!"

"Now you intrigue me. Show me your portrait."

Angelo stared at the painting, and marvelled at her beauty.

"She lives in a grand house with her long-suffering maid, saddened that she will never marry or know conjugal love."

"And she is perfect in all other respects?"

"Of course," Giovanni said with a smile. "And she has inherited wealth."

"Then I must meet the lady. I cannot smell a privy that would make the townsfolk retch, so her problem will not be a problem for me. Introduce me to her without delay."

Giovanni grumbled he had only left her that morning, but they finished the wine and made their way back to Isabella's house, with me following close behind.

The maid invited them in somewhat reluctantly, and told her mistress that Giovanni and his friend the picture–framer were waiting on her.

Isabella appeared, somewhat flustered.

"There was no need to bring your friend to see me, Giovanni," she said.

"On the contrary, Signorina, when I saw your portrait I insisted he brought me straight here."

With that he walked right up to her, took her hand and kissed it. She flushed, but he stood his ground, and they looked into each other's eyes. She was surprised and gratified that he was able to stand so close to her.

"Let me introduce myself. I am Angelo Giaconi, and I am delighted to meet you."

"And I am Isabella D'Adamo," she said, and she felt a thrill run though her body.

And then I felt a hand on my shoulder shaking me. I thought it was Giovanni, but remembered he couldn't see me. The hand shook more vigorously, and the gallery guard was looking at me.

"Are you all right, sir? You have been sitting here for the past hour without moving, so I thought I would come over and check."

I straightened myself up. "Yes, I'm fine," I mumbled.

Was I daydreaming, I wondered? How could I have fallen asleep on that bench?

I took one last look at Isabella's portrait. To my astonishment the sadness had gone from her face, and I could swear there was the vestige of a contented smile!

A Piece Of Chocolate

The white-haired man disembarked from the plane at Tempelhof Airport. He went through the usual formalities but did not wait by the carousel, as his sole luggage consisted of a holdall grip small enough to be allowed on the aircraft. He was born in Berlin, but had only vague memories of his early childhood there. It was strange hearing his first language spoken by everyone after all these years. Jacob was Jewish, and had lived in England since the end of the Second World War. He hailed a taxi to his hotel, but nothing he saw on the journey jogged his memory, or made any impression on him. The passing scene looked much the same as any other large city. The hotel receptionist greeted him with a smile, his room was comfortable, and everyone was helpful and polite.

Jacob sat in his room and made some phone calls. He had done most of his research in England, some of it with the help of the Internet, but he had to tie up some loose ends. The next day he went to the library and requested the telephone directory for the small town of Flamberg. He had a name, he had never forgotten it, and now he had a town. Although he had established a family connection between the individual and the town, it was a bit of a long shot as to whether Werner Mauser still lived there, or, indeed, whether he was still alive. On the positive side, however, the surname was not common, and he would not have to wade through pages of Schmidts and Schneiders. He struck lucky almost immediately. There were four Mausers, but only one whose forename began with W.

Jacob made a note of the address.

The next day he caught the train to Flamberg and booked into a small hotel. Although he was going to call on Herr Mauser, he had no intention of letting him know in advance. He soon established that he lived in a small flat that was part of a sheltered housing complex, and Jacob suddenly realised, in a way that he hadn't fully appreciated, that the man he intended visiting was well into his eighties. The warden, a large woman who had keys dangling at her belt like a jailer, was protective, and wanted to know who he was.

"A friend from long ago," Jacob said. "I have come a long way to see him."

She accompanied him to Werner's door, and reluctantly left them alone together. Werner walked with a stick, his head slumped forward and his back bent, as if his spine could no longer support his weight.

"Who are you? I don't know you," he said, when they were seated.

"But I know you," Jacob said. "I was in Dachau."

The old man looked at Jacob with watery eyes.

"I don't know what you are talking about. I was a soldier; I fought on the Eastern Front."

"Let me refresh your memory," Jacob replied. "It is perhaps understandable that you wish to forget the inhumanity in which you were an unwilling participant.

"It was 1942, and I was ten years old. We lived in a long, low building with many other women, and a few children. My father had been separated from us at the beginning, and we learned later that a guard had shot him, because he had answered back. My little sister was also taken away, and we never heard of her again. I could hardly remember what life was like before the camp. The daily routine, the searches - although we had little enough to hide, the certain death for those who could not work, the daily meal of watery soup and a piece of bread, the constant hunger, the smell of decay and dying, this was our life.

"Being young and foolhardy, I would sneak out and visit other parts of the camp, sometimes taking messages to husbands or relatives. Had I been caught, as young as I was, my life would not have been spared. I expected any day to have my relative freedom curtailed and to be put to work with the men. It was only because I looked younger than my years that I had not been moved to another part of the camp.

"For most of the guards, life was dull and full of routine. Except for the sadists, they were not deliberately cruel, but neither were they friendly. They were just completely indifferent to our plight. There was one soldier, however, who used to smile when he saw me and, one day, he ruffled my hair and said he had a son who was about my age. During the cold winter of that year, my mother fell ill. I stole a piece of bread for her, but she could not eat it.

"'Jacob,' she said, 'you must be brave; I am dying. Do not give up; you must survive so that you can be a witness to what has happened.'

"My mother died during the night and, the next morning, some soldiers came and unceremoniously carted her away, whilst I wept beside her empty bed, my face in the foul-smelling blanket.

"One of the guards, the one that had smiled at me, remained behind on some pretext and, when he was sure that no one was watching, he produced something from his greatcoat pocket and thrust it into my hand. He then quickly left to catch up with the others. I rubbed the tears from my eyes and looked at the object in my hand, which was wrapped in silver paper: it contained a large piece of chocolate. This was an unheard-of luxury, and I could not believe it. Before anyone could see, or ask for a piece, I stuffed it all into my mouth. Nothing has ever tasted so good: it was sheer bliss. That kindly action made me resolve to survive, and gave me the strength to keep going.

"That guard's name was Werner Mauser."

Werner was silent for a long time, and then he said,

"Those were terrible times. I did things for which I am ashamed, but I too could have been shot for disobeying orders."

"You took a risk with me," Jacob said, "and for that, I have never forgotten you."

Werner sighed.

"To tell you the truth," he said, "I don't remember the incident."

Mancurren

I first met Mancurren in the pub. After a couple of pints, he said,

"I'm terminal. Know what that means? I've got three months; at least that's what they say. It's approximate; could be more, could be less."

I did not look surprised. Don't get me wrong, you couldn't tell by looking at him; it was just that I'd known him for less than two hours. It's like when you hear about kids starving to death in Africa; it's bad, but you can't get emotional like it was someone close to you.

"It's the big C," he said, "I'm riddled with it."

He got out a packet of cigarettes and offered me one before lighting up.

"No need to worry about this now," he said, with a faint smile.

I told him my name was John, but he wouldn't enlarge on Mancurren.

We met occasionally after that. I would call in for a pint, and he would be sitting there in the corner. One day he said,

"Sometimes I don't feel like going out. I don't suppose you would come around, and we could have a few beers at my place?"

His place was a small council flat. You could tell it lacked a woman's touch, but he did not notice the mess, or the clutter.

"Have you no family?" I asked.

He smiled ruefully.

"I have a daughter somewhere, but I haven't seen her since she was a year old. She's probably got children of her own by now. As for her mother…" He didn't finish the sentence.

"I've probably got other kids I don't know about. I've been a bit of a rolling stone. There was one woman, though, her name was Amy; she was something else, we couldn't get enough of each other."

"What happened?"

"I felt trapped; buggered off in the end, but I regret that now. I can't even find a photo of her - must have lost it when I moved here. Do me a favour, will you? Get us a few things from the corner shop; I've made a list."

It was tinned stuff mostly, and some eggs. When I returned I said,

"Why don't you contact the Council, get them to provide you with one of them home helps?"

"No way," he said, "can't be bothered with any of that stuff. I don't want them busybodies prying around."

He picked up a can of beans.

"That's the wrong brand; I told you not this one."

He never said thanks, but getting his groceries became a regular thing after that. The crafty sod knew I wouldn't be able to say no. The next time I saw him he said,

"The doc wants me to go into one of them hospices. I watched a programme about them once – all them nuns creeping about the place. I told him I'm not interested in that religious stuff. He said I'd got it all wrong, they don't try to convert you, but I said it's not for me."

He'd been sitting in his armchair, when he suddenly doubled up in pain. When the spasm passed, Mancurren straightened up and took a few deep breaths.

"I could start a chemist shop with all the tablets I take, but none of them do any good."

Then he fished in his pocket and produced a key.

"This is a spare; you keep it for me, in case…"

"In case what?"

"Well I might be in bed or in the lav when you ring the bell."

I looked him in the eyes.

"You also might be dead!"

"That too," he said.

"Then I hope you have made some arrangements."

"Arrangements? What for?"

"You know; your funeral, of course."

"I haven't thought about it. I couldn't give a toss what happens to my body after I'm dead."

"Someone will have to dispose of you," I said. "They can't just chuck you in a landfill site!"

"Listen, my friend, when you are dead, that's it. You are gone, finished, kaput; it's over, you don't exist, the same as it was before your dad's sperm fused with your mother's egg."

He paused; "Well, all right then, I prefer cremation, but I don't want some bloke, or woman for that matter, spouting a load of crap over me. I don't want any ceremony; just take me to the crematorium and let them pull the lever, or whatever it is they do."

"I won't be taking you anywhere, I'm not an undertaker."

"No, but you can be my - what do they call it? – executor."

"I don't want to be your executor, but you ought to make a will."

He laughed.

"What for? I don't have any money, so you needn't think you will get something for keeping me company."

I didn't answer.

"In the past," Mancurren said, "I earned good money; I crewed on a millionaire's yacht, and worked for the rich and famous, but the more I earned the more I spent; on gambling, on women, on having a good time. I lived for the day, and wasn't concerned with the future, so I can't complain now."

Why don't you try and trace your daughter?" I said.

He was angry; I'd touched a nerve and for a moment I thought he was going to heave himself up out of the chair and aim a punch at me.

"It's too late now, far too late. I've never shown any interest, so how can I justify it now, because I'm dying? No way; no bloody way."

He stared at me moodily for a while; then his face took on a benign expression.

"Make us a cup of tea, will you?" he said.

When I gave the mug of tea to him he said,

"What do you call this, gnat's pee?"

I said nothing, and he drank it without further comment.

It was a week before I could see him again, and he said,

"I thought you weren't coming, that you had given up on me."

I brought with me a six-pack and, when I had poured out two glasses he said,

"Do you know what I miss most? The company of women. I love women; that's why I couldn't stick to just one. And I'll tell you something - I'd like one right now, for sex. One more before I die. Maybe that would do it, finish me off, that is."

He grinned.

"What a way to go! Better than being here on my own, or sitting here looking at your ugly mug."

I wasn't meant to take offence at this, but I said,

"My ugly mug is all you have at present, so you can take it, or leave it."

He ignored that and said,

"I dreamed about Amy last night. She was the one I loved the most.

'Why did you leave me?' she asked. 'We were so right for each other.'

"I couldn't' give her an answer.

'We could have been happy,' she whispered, 'but that was long ago, and now I am married and have a family.'"

The next time I called he was in bed. He shouted for me to let myself in, and this caused him to have a coughing fit. When he had recovered he said,

"The doc called this morning. A nurse is going to come each day to give me an injection of morphine. I said why not just leave the stuff here, and I'll inject myself, but he won't do it - thinks I'll take an overdose."

I was with him for a couple of hours, and he spent most of the time reminiscing about his early life. Then he got out his wallet.

"Go down to the off-licence for me, will you, and get me a bottle of malt? *Glenfiddich*, if they have it."

"Are you sure you should be drinking whisky on top of morphine, and all that other stuff you take?"

"I'm as sure as I'll ever be," he said. "Now hurry up and get me that whisky."

When I returned he said thank you for the first time since I had known him.

I had a feeling he was going to end it. He was going downhill, and he was in pain, so why prolong the agony? I didn't see it as my job to stop him; I hadn't the right to do that but, all the same, I felt uneasy, and had a restless night. Next morning, I got up early and went to his flat. I rang the bell, and let myself in with his key. He wasn't in the living room or the kitchen, and so I went into the bedroom. There he was sitting up in bed, his eyes half-open, the empty whisky bottle and an assortment of pills scattered over the top of his bedside cabinet. I bent over him, but could not detect any breathing; he was obviously dead. I phoned his GP, who told me whom else I should notify, and he also arranged for an ambulance to take Mancurren away. There was a post mortem, but eventually the body was released to the undertaker and I made sure that his wishes regarding the disposal of his body were carried out. Then I had a phone call from the Housing Department. The official said they had been unable to trace any relatives and, as I had been his friend, would I accompany her to go through his things so that they could clear the flat for another tenant? We shredded his old bills, letters and papers, after checking that none contained any clues that would lead us to his next of kin, and bagged any serviceable clothes for the charity shop. She glanced around at the furniture.

"There's nothing of value here," she said. "A colleague will come with a van tomorrow and take the rest of the stuff to the dump."

I picked up a paperback that had fallen on the floor, and a photo fell out from between its pages. It was of a smiling young woman and, on the back, it said, "To Albert with all my love, Amy."

"So that was his first name."

"Pardon?" the housing official said.

"Nothing," I replied. "Do you mind if I keep this?"

"Be my guest," she said.

A Good Deed

I was sitting at my writing desk looking at a blank sheet of paper. My pen was poised ready to glide over the smooth surface; it had been poised for the last twenty minutes, but without effect. I have this urge to write a short story; I know I can write one, but there is a problem – I haven't an idea in my head, my mind is a complete blank. What a failure of the imagination, I tell myself as I put the pen down on the oak desk. I like my desk, it is solid, Victorian, with three drawers either side of the kneehole. It's also in keeping with the room; deep-upholstered leather armchairs, a small dining-table and wood panelling that I had installed when I moved in. The effect is a bit like a gentleman's club; my ex-wife would definitely not approve, but then, if our tastes had been more compatible, we would still be together.

I got up and looked out of the window. I have a good view of the street from my second-floor apartment; it's not a busy thoroughfare, but neither is it a quiet, suburban backwater. There are some local shops, including a convenience store, and a ladies' hairdresser, and we are on a bus route. I could see a few pedestrians, and some cars parked outside the shops. A young woman was walking slowly along the pavement opposite. As she approached two men coming towards her she put one hand up to her head, staggered a few paces, and fell to the ground.

The men ran the few yards to where she was lying and bent over her. I hesitated for a few seconds, then rushed out of my flat, sprinted down two flights of stairs, and arrived at the scene breathing heavily. If the girl had fainted, she now seemed to have recovered consciousness.

One of the men was saying,

"Shall I call an ambulance?"

"No, no," the girl said, "don't do that. I'll be all right."

The man seemed doubtful. She was now sitting up on the pavement and so I helped her to her feet.

"I'm fine, really," she said, "I just need to sit down and rest for a few minutes."

"I live just across the road," I said. "You can rest in my flat if you like."

"Thanks," the girl said, noticing me for the first time, "I'll take you up on that."

The two men looked relieved and went on their way, whilst the girl and I crossed the road and went up in the lift to my apartment. I offered her a cup of tea and she accepted. Through the open kitchen door I could see her having a good look around the room. She seemed to have recovered from her collapse remarkably quickly. I placed her tea on a side table.

"My name is Jason," I said.

"Mine's Lynne."

She drank her tea and stood up, dropping her canvas shoulder bag on the carpet. It was the first time I'd had a good look at her. I guessed she was in her early twenties. Her brown hair was tied back in a ponytail, and her thin body was encased in a tee-shirt and tight, scruffy jeans moulded to the shape of her small, round bottom. If it wasn't for the swelling of her breasts she could have been mistaken for a young man.

"You've got a nice place here," she said.

"I like it," I replied. "Are you feeling better?

"Yes, I think so."

"Is there anyone you want to phone?"

I pointed to the telephone on my desk.

"No, not really."

There was a pause while I waited for her to say that it was time she went.

"Don't mind me asking," she said, "but have you got anything to eat?"

"Eat?" I said, puzzled. "Are you hungry?"

"Yes I am; I haven't eaten since yesterday."

"Well, in that case, will an omelette do?"

"Yeah, that's fine."

While I busied myself in the kitchen, I wondered about her. Was she living with her parents? Somehow I doubted it - probably had a bed-sit somewhere. She devoured the omelette with several slices of bread, and a piece of apple pie I had been keeping to have myself later.

"Where do you live?" I asked her.

"I don't. I don't live anywhere, that is."

I began to feel uneasy.

You mean you are homeless?"

"That's about it."

"You must have been staying somewhere."

"For the last week I have been staying at a friend's place, but her boyfriend turned me out this morning and told me not to come back, or he'd thump me. I didn't even have time to collect the rest of my clothes."

"And before that?"

"Do you really want my life story? Look, thanks for the meal but I had better be going." She picked up her bag.

"Wait," I said. "Where are you staying tonight?"

"How the hell do I know?" she said irritably.

"If I let you stay here tonight," I heard myself saying, "will you go to Social Services and explain your situation, so they can find you a place in a hostel?"

"Yeah, all right," she said.

Immediately I regretted opening my mouth. What had I let myself in for, I wondered? I made a meal for us both that evening and, between mouthfuls, she told me that she had been brought up in a children's home. Her mother had died when she was two, and she had no idea who her father was. She had been living with someone for a while but when he was evicted they had split up. This did not bother her, as he was always stoned out of his head.

"You will have to sleep in here," I said.

We were eating in my living room.

"I'll give you a duvet and a couple of pillows."

I thought she would use the leather two-seater, but she said the floor was fine. In bed that night I asked myself why I always fell for a hard-luck story. I had realised that I was stuck with her for another day, as the next day was Sunday and the Social Services office would be closed.

In the morning I went into the living room to open the curtains. She was lying there with the duvet wrapped around her. Her jeans and tee-shirt were on the carpet.

"Hiya," she said, and sat up, exposing her breasts. Then she stood up naked and came towards me.

"I owe you," she said, loosening the tie of my bathrobe.

Now I'm no monk, but the last thing I wanted was to get involved with this rootless girl whom I had met less than 24 hours earlier. I was doing a good deed, for God's sake, and I wanted her out as quickly as possible.

"No," I said, removing her hands.

She didn't seem to understand. "What do you want me to do?"

"I want you to have a shower, and get dressed."

"Have it your way." She was angry.

"You're not gay, are you?"

I tightened my grip on her wrists. Suddenly her anger dissipated and she laughed out loud.

She disrupted my Sunday, and kept asking questions. What did I do for a living? Did I have a mother? Why did my marriage break up (she'd seen a photo of my ex)? And would I like to smoke a joint? She hadn't any of the stuff on her but, if I gave her some money, she knew where she could get some. She looked in my drinks cabinet and asked if she could have some vodka, and then proceeded to put away an amount that would have had me under the table.

It was with a sigh of relief that I dropped her off at Social Services on the way to my office.

"Good luck, Lynne," I said, pressing a fiver into her hand.

When I arrived home that evening she was sitting on the step by the entry phone.

"What happened?" I said.

"Nothing; I saw a social worker called Tina. She said that as I had a temporary address she would make some enquiries about accommodation, and let me know on Wednesday. I also went to the benefits office and tried to get some money – it's easier when you have an address – and they are going to send me a Giro."

"This is getting beyond a joke," I said. "Just because I let you sleep on the floor overnight doesn't give you the right to call my home your temporary address."

"I didn't call it that, Tina did!"

I opened the door, and she followed me in.

The next day I was very busy at the office, and I had to leave Lynne alone in the flat to await a call from the social worker.

When I arrived home that evening I could smell burning.

"Hi Jason," she said.

I ignored the greeting and walked straight into the kitchen.

"What's that I can smell?"

There were a couple of blackened pans on the stove, containing the burnt remains of some vegetables. She followed me in, and I could smell gin on her breath; she'd been at my drinks again.

"I thought I would make us dinner," she said, "But I forgot all about them; I'm sorry."

The next morning I called at Social Services on my way to work and demanded to see Tina. I told her I'd come about Lynne, and realised I didn't even know her surname.

"Ah yes," Tina said; "The girl has a lot of problems, but I can't discuss them with you - it's confidential."

"I don't want to discuss her problems; I just want her out of my flat."

"In that case," the young social worker said, "Why did you let her in? Perhaps you had an ulterior motive and, when she wouldn't play ball..."

I could have hit her, but I composed myself and said,

"What are you doing about finding her accommodation?"

"I have been making inquiries," she said. "There are a number of voluntary agencies that cater for homeless women, but it's finding the right placement that's the problem, and then, of course, whether they have a vacancy."

"I thought local authorities had a responsibility for the homeless," I said.

"Only if there are children," she replied.

"So how long will it be before you find her somewhere?"

"I can't say; hopefully within the next few weeks."

"A few weeks! That's not good enough."

"You could always tell her to take her things and go; we would do our best to find her somewhere for the night."

"She hasn't any things, and she is waiting to receive a Giro cheque; but what if she won't go?"

Tina shrugged.

"I'm not a lawyer."

"Then I'll have to consult one," I said.

Back at the office I phoned Jack; he's a partner in a law firm and I'd known him from childhood.

"You and your good deeds," he said. "You always were a sucker for a hard-luck story."

"But what shall I do?" I asked.

"Well, as the social worker said, you could evict her – by force if necessary, but then you would lay yourself open to a charge of assault. You could also phone the police and say you have a trespasser, an uninvited guest who refuses to leave your flat. They will be reluctant to get involved but, if they do send a constable to escort her from the premises, he couldn't stop her hanging around outside and pestering you to let her stay a while longer. If she persisted, you would need a court order to stop that!"

When I arrived home she was wearing my bathrobe.

"I've washed my clothes," she said. "They're in the dryer."

She was lounging on the settee with two bags beside her.

"My Giro arrived today, Jason, so I went out and bought some stuff I needed."

"How did you get back in?"

She smiled.

"I found your spare key in the kitchen drawer."

"Then can I have it back, please?"

She rummaged around in one of her bags and gave it back reluctantly.

"We must have a serious talk this evening, Lynne," I said.

"Why have we got to be serious?" she said and, throwing off my robe, she walked into the kitchen to retrieve her clothes.

After we had eaten I told her that she must go the following day and that, if she didn't, I would call the police to help me evict her.

She laughed.

"The fuzz; would you really?" Then, seeing my expression, she said,

"Yes, I think you mean it; what a pity, I like it here and I like you, even though you don't find me sexy."

"That's not the point," I said lamely. "Whether I think you are attractive is neither here nor there."

Next morning, I gave her a small rucksack to put her things in and said it was time we were going.

"Would you do me one last favour?" she asked.

"What is that?"

"Take me t Hampstead."

"Why Hampstead? Aren't you going to see Tina?"

"No."

I was a bit worried about this and, as we were driving there I asked her again, but all she would say was that there were some nice people in Hampstead.

"And some rich ones," I added.

We drove up Haverstock Hill and suddenly she said,

"Turn right," and then, "Stop here."

"Are you sure?" I said.

"Yes, this is fine."

"Well," I said awkwardly, "I hope you know what you are doing; take care, Lynne."

She put her hand on my arm and said,

"Thanks for all that you did," and slammed the car door shut.

I was feeling guilty, God knows why, and I sat in the car as she walked up the road. There were some pedestrians about and, as Lynne drew near some of them, she put her hand to her head and collapsed onto the pavement. I was horrified; she was trying that trick again. Surely none of those people would be taken in by it, the way I had been? I turned on the ignition and pressed hard on the accelerator; I wasn't going to stop to find out!

When I arrived home that day I surveyed my living room; it was in a mess. I hadn't realised until now how untidy she had made the place. I would have to give it a good clean. I could see something sticking out from under the back of the settee. I pulled it out and held it up; it was a pair of knickers. On my desk were two used coffee cups, one of them on my A4 pad that was stained with coffee. Tearing off the top sheet I sat down at the desk, took out my pen and wrote the following:

I wanted to write a short story, but I didn't have an idea in my head, then I stood up and looked out of the window...

An Eventful Day

S usie pushed the buggy along the wet pavement. It had been raining, but now the sun had come out, a warm, invigorating sun that made steam rise from the cracked paving, and the run-down, poorer part of town in which she lived seem less depressing. Past the betting shop and the chippy, past the Chinese takeaway, and Sanjay at the corner store taking his steel shutters down, and heading for the park. Not the rec with its broken swings, but the big park in the town centre. It was a long walk, but the sky was blue and there was a spring in her step. Little Ben, just six months old, was enjoying himself too, because every so often he gave a happy gurgle.

There was another reason for going to Jubilee Park, the official name of this civic homage to Victoria's long reign, and that was the announcement of a festival on this Saturday morning.

As they neared the grand entrance, massive, wrought-iron gates that were flung wide open, they encountered others all going in the same direction - mothers with pushchairs, children with their parents, and even teenagers. There was a sense of excitement in the air and, although not yet noon, the park was already crowded. Dogs barked, a brass band played on the Victorian bandstand, kids rode high on their dads' shoulders, and families were already spreading blankets in preparation for a picnic.

Susie pushed the buggy past the ice-cream seller, and did not stop until she came to a little refreshment pavilion with tables and chairs outside. Parking Ben at one of the few vacant tables near to the serving counter, and keeping one eye on him, she bought herself a cup of tea. She took a sip of the strong, sweet tea and then, seized by a sudden rush of love, took Ben out of his pushchair and stood him on her knees. She bounced him and she cooed at him, she made snorting noises to amuse him, and then rubbed her nose against him. Finally, she hugged him and smothered him with kisses.

A couple at the next table smiled at her uninhibited demonstration of affection. Ben frowned and put his fingers in his mouth, a sign that he was hungry, so she took his bottle out of her bag and fed him. When he was satisfied, she delved again and took out the sandwich that she had hurriedly prepared earlier for herself.

Then it was time to look around the festival, for there was plenty to see. Susie put Ben back in his buggy and pulled the back up to shield him from the now-hot sun.

Craftsmen, vendors and local organisations had put up their tents, awnings and stalls, and these were spread widely over the soft, green grass.

She stopped to admire a wood-worker shaping a stool from green wood. She could smell the earthy leaf litter and tannin scent of the shavings as he worked. He had items for sale, but no one was buying; they were too busy watching, mesmerised as he used his few simple tools to such good effect. Ben waved a tiny arm at him as they moved on.

She passed a group of teenagers larking, flirting and drinking coke. One threw an empty can on the grass. She wanted to say something, or alternatively pick it up, but she did neither - it was too nice a day to be confrontational.

Down a grassy bank and they watched two puppies play-fighting each other, learning deep skills from their wolf ancestors, while Ben bobbed up and down with excitement and wonder. She herself felt the day had a dreamlike quality, with her and Ben in their own little world viewing all sorts of magical things happening around them.

In the distance a figure, high in the air, suspended under a massive oak.

They moved closer; a girl in a leotard was hanging from a thin strip of fabric attached to a branch some thirty feet up, a ribbon of silk as a prop for her acrobatics, swinging, spiralling, appearing to fall yet not falling, and twisting the fabric around her lithe legs to hang head downwards. Mothers, fathers, children and friends were sitting on the grass watching. The girl slithered to the ground, and Susie clapped appreciatively.

There was still much to see, but she was thirsty again, so when she saw a tent advertising homemade cordials she had a closer look. The lady who had made these drinks was doing a brisk trade, so much so that it was difficult to see what she has set out on her trestle table, so she put the brake on the buggy and went inside. The reason for the crush then became apparent; she was giving out free drinks in the hope that the tasters would like it sufficiently to buy a bottle. Susie drank a plastic beaker of rhubarb cordial, and she would have bought some but there was a queue waiting to be served, so she squeezed through the cordial-tasters, back to little Ben - except he wasn't there.

Susie stared in disbelief at the spot where the pushchair had been, then she looked in all directions, but there was no sign of him. She began to panic, and she could feel her heart thumping.

"Have you seen a little boy in a pushchair?" she asked people standing around, but nobody had. She wanted to run, to search, but which way should she go?

There must be someone who can help, she told herself; she should tell a policeman, except she hadn't seen one. The dream-like quality of the day evaporated. The harsh reality was that Ben had disappeared, and all that mattered now was getting him back.

There was another awning with a lady seated behind a table. It was *Friends of the Earth* looking for new members. She looked bored. Susie ran to her.

"I've lost my little boy; where can I get help? Who should I tell?"

"There is a lost-and-found tent, maybe someone has taken him there. It's near the main gate. Don't worry, I'm sure you'll find him," she said reassuringly. Susie ran with unaccustomed energy, taking great gulps of air. Her mouth was dry and her stomach felt as if small insects were biting her from within.

She arrived at the tent breathless, but there was no sign of Ben.

She explained about Ben to the woman in charge of the phones and other lost items.

"I only left him for a minute," she said tearfully.

"I can't leave this place unattended," the woman said, "but there is a loudspeaker at the bandstand; they will make an announcement, ask anyone who has found Ben to bring him there. If that doesn't work you will have to call the police."

Susie felt sick. She was just about to make her way to the bandstand when she spotted a woman and a boy about ten years old walking towards her. The boy and his mother were each wheeling identical pushchairs. She ran to meet them and saw that the boy was pushing Ben.

"Ben," she said, scooping him out of the chair and holding him to her, "Oh Ben."

Ben did not appear to be unduly distressed, but when he caught sight of his mother his face lit up.

"I am so sorry," the lady said. "It's all my stupid son's fault; he said he was going to watch the gymnasts while I was queuing for some cordial. We arranged to meet at the café, but the gymnasts were having a break, so he came back. He couldn't see me, so the silly boy pushed your Ben to the cafe without checking. I can't imagine what he was thinking - as if I would leave Ryan on his own!"

Overcome with relief, Susie said,

"If only I had had the hood down he would have noticed, but the sun was so strong."

"I wouldn't count on it," she said, still angry with her son.

When they were alone Susie said to Ben, "I think it's time we went home."

Ben bounced in his chair. He was looking at a pigeon pecking at the remains of a hamburger. Susie looked in her purse and checked the contents. It was the bus home or the corner store, but not both. She decided they would walk, and set off at a brisk pace, but soon slowed down. She was becoming tired and couldn't wait to get back to their little flat. The route was familiar, and at first she didn't notice the man, whom she later thought was in his fifties, come lurching towards them. As soon as she had looked directly at him Susie knew it was a mistake. As they drew level he impeded her progress and touched his forehead in a mock salute.

"Is this the way to…?"

His voice trailed off. He seemed to have forgotten where he thought the road might lead, or where he wanted to go. He just stood there swaying, and then he bent forward, grabbing Susie for support, and exhaled a beery breath on Ben, who wrinkled his nose.

"Canny lad there, missis," he slurred, and she thought he looked sad.

"Yes," she said, removing an arthritic hand from her arm, and trying to push forward.

"Wass the hurry? Somethin' wrong?"

"I want to go home, please let me pass."

She pushed forward, and he reluctantly stepped aside. She hurried on as he shouted incoherently after her.

At Sanjay's she went straight to the chilled cabinet and took out curried chicken and rice for one. It seemed a bit small, but she could not afford the larger size. A few minutes later she was turning the key to her flat. She put her dinner in the oven to heat and fed Ben. Then she spooned the heated meal onto a plate, with an extra slice of bread, and turned the television on. Sitting in a comfortable chair with the meal on her lap, she relaxed contentedly. It had been an eventful day; tomorrow would be ordinary.

The Blue Uniform

Y ou may find my story hard to believe, but I have it on good authority that it is true. A friend, who had it from the man who was the village priest at the time, told it to me. These events took place in an age when country folk were less sophisticated than they are in this modern age.

This is what the old priest told my friend.

In a little town in Ireland in the early 1920s there lived a ne'er-do-well, small-time gambler and dealer in shady goods, called Malloy. He had chosen to live in that place because of its proximity to a racecourse, but he had suffered a run of exceptionally bad luck and he was so far behind with his rent that his landlady had given him notice to leave the very next day, having given up all hope of getting the money due to her.

Malloy did not know what he was going to do, or where he would go, but he decided to spend his last day at the races. He fancied a horse called Mickey's Boy and he was sure that it was going to be his lucky day. He put five shillings on to win at 20 to 1, and waited anxiously for the race to begin. His horse ran a good race lying fourth most of the way, and then putting on a spurt nudged ahead just before the finish. Malloy heaved a sigh of relief, and his spirits rose. He headed for his favourite pub, and had a few pints of

Guinness. Feeling in even better spirits, he went to see Rafferty, the owner of a second-hand shop, with whom he frequently did business. He peered into the dusty window and saw, draped over an old tailor's dummy, the most amazing uniform he had ever seen. It was royal blue, with shiny brass buttons and gold braid. There were medal ribbons, epaulettes with insignia, and a peaked cap. Malloy went inside.

"How's yourself then, Rafferty?" he said, beaming.

Rafferty looked at him quizzically.

"I see you have nothing for me today," he said, with the air of a man with no time to waste, "so what would you be wanting, then?"

Malloy pointed at the uniform. "Where did you get that?"

"None of your business, Mister Malloy, but it's top quality sure enough."

"Reckon it was made for some big shot, an ambassador or admiral, I'd guess," Malloy said.

More like a commissionaire, thought Rafferty, but he said,

"A very high-class person, to be sure. I'll get a good price for it. In fact, I'm thinking of hiring it out for fancy-dress parties."

"Fancy dress? In this town?" said Malloy incredulously.

"I'll give you ten bob for it."

Rafferty looked hurt. "You're having me on; I wouldn't part with it for under £2 at least."

The two men haggled but, in the end, they settled on one pound and five shillings. Malloy thought Rafferty had driven a hard bargain.

Back in his room he stroked the cloth lovingly, and couldn't wait to try it on. It fitted to perfection, and he admired his reflection in the cracked mirror. Stretching his body to stand as high as he could, Malloy felt different, important even.

The next morning, he dressed in his uniform and put his few belongings in a small, cardboard suitcase. His landlady was affronted.

"Wasting your money on uniforms when you owe me rent," she screamed. "Pay me, you trickster."

"I will. So I will, missis, as soon as I get myself straight."

The landlady snorted. "Goodbye and good riddance," she said, as she closed the front door on him.

Malloy was undecided what to do, although he thought it was probably time for him to move on to another town. As he walked down the road, whom should he see but Liam McArthur, the bookie, driving towards him. Motorcars were not all that common in the west of Ireland at this time; that he should own one at all was newsworthy, but this one was shiny and spanking-new. In the ordinary way he wouldn't have stopped to pass the time of day with Malloy, but the sight of him in his resplendent blue uniform was too much. McArthur pulled up beside him with a squeal of brakes.

"Where do you think you're going in that outfit?"

Malloy did not answer the question. Instead he said,

"That's a handsome motor you have there, mister."

Then he pointed to the luggage on the dickey seat.

"Off on holiday then, is it?"

"Going touring," McArthur said, "to run-in my new motorcar."

"Can I come with you?"

"You must be joking."

"I'll pay you to give me a lift then," Malloy said.

McArthur thought for a moment. He didn't like the man, but he could always drop him off when he'd had enough of his company. And he hadn't made his money by refusing cash when it was offered.

They travelled through deserted lanes, passing only the occasional farm cart, and a tinker's caravan, the horse quietly munching grass until startled by the sound of the engine. Malloy kept up a continuous commentary on the passing scene and McArthur who, despite his profession, was a contemplative type, wished he had not agreed to the arrangement. He resolved to get rid of Malloy at the earliest opportunity so, when they reached a poor-looking place with humble cottages, a church, a little shop and a scruffy-looking pub called the *Brendan Arms*, McArthur came to a halt.

"This is as far as you go," he said to Malloy.

"What do you mean? Are you staying in this Godforsaken place?"

"No, but you are."

"I paid good money."

"Yes, but this is as far as it will take you," he said, throwing out Malloy's case.

Malloy got out of the motor to retrieve it as a group of locals gathered to marvel at the sight of a motor vehicle from which a man in an important-looking blue uniform stepped down. There is some dispute about what happened next, but the retired priest who related the story to my friend thought that McArthur said in jest before driving off,

"Take good care of the commissionaire," but the locals heard this as, "Take good care of the commissioner."

Whatever the truth of the matter the villagers, having learned that a man in a gold-braided uniform had arrived in Kilgare in a shiny new motorcar, were very impressed, and understood they were instructed to take care of their guest.

Malloy walked into the *Brendan Arms* still seething over his treatment by McArthur, and ordered a pint. The landlord carefully wiped the counter before placing the glass of stout down in front of him.

"And what would you be doing in these parts, Commissioner sir? You surely haven't come all the way from Dublin to see us folk?"

Malloy was impressed. He'd never been called "Commissioner sir" before, and he liked the sound of it. He did not contradict the suggestion that he was from Dublin.

"Have you a room?"

Few strangers ever stayed at the little village of Kilgare, but it so happened that the landlord, whose name was Hegarty, had a spare room owing to his son having recently gone to England to look for work.

"That I have, your worship, and it's a fine room to be sure. If I can make so bold, what business brings you to Kilgare?"

Malloy sensed that if he played his cards right he could use the situation to his advantage.

"Government business," he said, mysteriously.

The landlord persisted.

"If you wish to see Father O'Malley, it's a shame but you've just missed him. It was only this morning that he left to bury his old mother – may she rest in peace. His last words were that he would for sure be back next Sunday to take Mass."

Malloy was inspired.

"No. Not the priest, leastways not specially; I'm here to speak to ordinary people."

And so it was that the word soon spread that the government had sent a Commissioner to visit their small community to hear first-hand the problems that beset them. Malloy was treated like royalty. Drinks and accommodation were on the house, although the landlord totted up the amount just in case there was some way of recouping his loss. For the first few days the villagers came to him at the *Brendan Arms*, where he held court. They told him all their troubles: about the absentee landlord who would do nothing to repair their damp and crumbling cottages, about the lack of employment, about small farmers scratching a living from stony soil. They brought him food for his supper although they could ill afford it, and went without themselves as a consequence. At first he just listened, and made sympathetic noises but, after he had visited a family of eight living in a tiny hovel, in which a little girl was ill in the bed she shared with her three sisters, he began making positive statements. He would report back to the authorities and something would be done. As the week progressed his statements became wilder. When he discovered an illicit still at the back of the pub, a discovery that frightened the life out of the landlord, he said he would recommend that the production be legitimised so that it could be expanded to provide local employment. Fine labels would be put on the bottles and, in time, the brand would become as famous as *Jameson's*. Malloy was carried away by his own rhetoric and by the role he had created for himself.

Father O'Malley arrived back in the village late on Saturday night. Tired out, he went straight to bed in order to be up early for Mass. The next morning the landlord of the *Brendan Arms* knocked politely on Malloy's door and asked if he was going to church. Malloy grunted that he had a headache, and that was not surprising because he'd had quite a few pints the night before. Thus it was that Father O'Malley learned from his congregation the good news.

"Are you completely mad, Mr Hegarty?" he said to the landlord. "Villages such as ours don't receive visits from government officials, with or without fancy uniforms." Later he announced sternly from the pulpit,

"It has come to my notice that a gentleman – if we may call him that - has arrived in this village purporting to be a representative of the government, and that you have given him hospitality that you can ill afford. What is much worse, you have believed his lies about improving your lot. Only God can improve your lot through salvation. Attend to your devotions and do not listen to false Messiahs and confidence tricksters. We are a God-fearing community not versed in the sinful ways of the cities, so let this be a lesson to you all."

When the villagers returned from church they assembled in and around the *Brendan Arms*. Malloy was still in his room, sleeping off his hangover. Quietly they removed his uniform and the suitcase containing his other clothes and replaced them with a pair of trousers, a shirt and a jacket that were so patched and threadbare they were little better than rags. Malloy awoke to a room full of hostile people.

Intimidated, he came clean, but tried to put the blame on their credulity. He was made to put on the rags provided and frog-marched into the street then, shouting and jeering, they ran him out of the village and into the lonely countryside. If he ever set foot in the village again, they said, he would live to regret it.

"What happened to Malloy?" I asked my friend.

Apparently he disappeared and was never heard of again."

"And the uniform?"

The priest said he made Hegarty hang it behind the bar as a constant reminder of their gullibility, but that, too, disappeared after a while, and nobody wanted to enquire as to where it had gone.

The Two Friends

L inda sighed. She was just finishing her evening meal of boiled potatoes and a solitary, tasteless sausage, when the plaintive wail of the siren filled the air. She lived alone in a first-floor maisonette, and it wasn't safe to remain there during an air raid. A similar property in the next street had been completely demolished by a bomb the previous week.

She was tired, and reluctant to move after a long day at the factory and a freezing bus journey home. She was sitting there in her coat because she was saving her coal for the weekend, when she heard the sound of anti-aircraft fire. Another sleepless night, she thought, and grabbed her thick travelling blanket. The sky was ablaze with searchlights as she hurried to the communal shelter at the end of the street. The squat, reinforced-concrete building situated on what, before the war, had been a children's playground was a dismal place to spend the night. A row of two-tier bunks along one wall, a solitary lavatory best used only if one were desperate, and a few bare light-bulbs hanging from the ceiling casting a dim light on the women and children, and the few old men, who were sitting or lying on their bunks. Linda found a vacant lower bunk and sat down on the edge, head hunched forward to avoid hitting it on the upper tier. The mattress had a damp, musty smell and she was reluctant to lie on it full-length. She hoped the 'All-

Clear' would go soon, so she could get back home, fill her hot-water bottle and get into a warm bed. She wrapped her blanket around her and fantasised about luxuriating in a deep, hot bath.

Suddenly a pair of legs appeared from above, and a young woman slid down beside her.

"Bleeding place; it stinks in 'ere, don't it?"

She was a pretty blonde, hair done in the style of Veronica Lake. She recognised her as a girl who worked in the Dispatch Department at the factory.

Linda smiled.

"It's no home from home, but it's safe."

The girl pushed hair out of her eye.

"My name's Peggy; what's yours?"

"Linda. I've seen you in Dispatch."

"Yeah, well it's better than workin' on one of them lathes. Ain't seen you before, though."

"Lathes aren't so bad," Linda said. "It's hard work, though."

The girl reached up to the top bunk and retrieved a flask.

"Like some tea? You'll have to share me cup."

"Yes please." She had been in such a hurry she hadn't had time to make up a flask herself.

She insisted on Peggy drinking first then, when she had poured some out for her, said, "Where do you live, Peggy?"

"Just around the corner, in one of them little terraces in Grafton Street."

"All on your own?"

"Me dad's in the Army, and me mum's away in the country because she can't stand the bombing. She wanted me to come with her, but I said I'm not going out in the sticks.

She keeps writing and asking me to join her, but I like my job, leastways when Mr Ryan is not pestering me."

"Mr Ryan? Isn't he the office manager?"

"That's right; he keeps coming up behind me, and putting his arm around me pretending he's interested in my work, the creep, and he's started calling me into his office just before the whistle goes and saying he knows a nice pub, and he'd like to buy me a drink."

"What do you say?"

I pretend my mum's at home, and she's expecting me. There aint nothin' I can do about it; I can't go over his head and, even if I could, they wouldn't listen; they'd just say I should stop making a fuss."

Linda sympathized; "He's married, of course."

"Goes without saying; how about you?" Peggy said.

Linda drained the last of the tea.

"Yes, I'm married; his name is Geoffrey and he's in the Army out in North Africa somewhere."

"You must miss him."

"The funny thing is I don't miss him all that much. I can hardly remember what he was like. The thing is, we hadn't been going out that long when he received a posting. It was all very quick; he persuaded me to marry him, we had a few days together, then he was gone."

Suddenly, there were several loud thumps and the anti-aircraft barrage increased in volume. Some people who had been lying down sat up, and two young children woke and started to cry. Peggy nervously screwed the top back on her flask and they sat silently, listening to the crashing and banging going on outside. Eventually the noise ceased and the 'All-Clear' sounded. It was two o'clock. Linda said,

"Shall I walk home with you?"

The young woman shook her head.

"No, you get to your bed; I'll be all right, really I will."

She left her at the corner of Grafton Street, part of which was cordoned off because the front of someone's house had caved in.

"One of our own shells," a man said, "They don't always explode on their targets."

Her alarm clock went off at six thirty next morning, and Linda dragged herself wearily out of bed.

During the lunch break she caught up with Peggy in the canteen.

"You look tired," she said to Linda.

"I could sleep for a week but, if there's a raid tonight, let's keep each other company."

That evening the Luftwaffe had a night off and, it being the warmest place, she went to bed early. It was a brief respite though, because, on the following evening she saw flashes in the night sky even before the siren sounded, and she hastened to the shelter, where she met up with Peggy.

Her friend was subdued; her quick, Cockney wit seemed to have deserted her.

"What's up, Peggy?" Linda said, "You're very quiet tonight."

"I don't know; everything seems to be getting on top of me. Mum wrote again asking me to join her, and saying that I would have no trouble getting a farm job as they are very short-handed." She gave a faint smile.

"Can you see me as a bloody milkmaid? And on top of that, Mr Ryan is still trying it on with me. If he puts his arms around me once more I'll, I'll…." She was lost for words.

"Kick him in the balls?" Linda suggested, and they both laughed.

Peggy relaxed a little; she wanted to unburden herself to Linda.

"I nearly packed it in last week after we had that choking fog; smog, the papers called it. The bus driver turned us off; said he would have an accident if he went any further. It was getting dark and it was so dense I couldn't see a foot in front of me!"

"I'm not surprised," Linda said, "I wasn't able to get home at all, and had to bed down at the factory."

"I kept bumping into lamp-posts, and wondered how I was going to get home; then I heard footsteps behind me, so I stopped, and they stopped, and I said, 'Hello, can you help me?' but there was no answer and, when I started walking again, so did they. I was petrified."

Linda laid a reassuring hand on her friend.

"What did you do?"

"I saw a faint light coming from a doorway; it was the *Quick Stop Café*, and so I knew where I was. Lucky for me my neighbour, Tess, was inside, so we had some tea, then linked arms and found our way home."

She had just stopped talking when the barrage began in earnest. The sound of anti-aircraft fire was interspersed with loud explosions that made the ground shake. The noise rumbled on but gradually became quieter, and they lay on their bunks, trying to get some sleep. They spent the rest of the night in the shelter and emerged the next morning to a scene of devastation. There were fire engines and heavy-rescue vehicles in the streets. Dazed people in shock were being cared for by St John Ambulance men.

Grafton Street had received a direct hit and was closed to all but the rescue workers. They spoke to a Civil Defence man, who confirmed that Peggy's house had been demolished. Linda comforted Peggy and took her back to the maisonette, thankfully undamaged apart from some broken windows.

"Everything's gone," she said, in tears, "I've got nothing except the clothes I'm wearing."

"You've got your life," Linda said. "We can get you some more clothes, and we may be able to salvage some stuff from the rubble."

"I'll have to go to Mum's now."

"You don't have to; you can stay here. I've got the room. We can keep each other company."

"What about Geoff?"

"What about him? I'll write and tell him."

"I'd better phone my mum and tell her the bad news."

"I heard one of the men say the phone lines are all down, but you can send her a telegram; now, let's make some tea."

During the next week there were intermittent raids, and the friends spent several nights in the shelter. This was followed by a quiet spell, and it coincided with Linda being asked to go on the night shift, a change she could not refuse.

Then one night there was a heavy raid and the workers on her shift had to take cover until it was over. For the rest of the night she worried about Peggy; would she go to the shelter? She certainly hoped so. The bus home had to make a detour due to a bomb crater in the road, and the conductor said, "Have you heard? The shelter in Victoria Street recreation ground got a direct hit. They think it was a land mine. My mate said there were many casualties. What's the point of going, I say; you may as well stay at home and take your chances." But Linda had stopped listening; she was praying that Peggy had not gone to the shelter the previous night. Running from the bus stop, she turned the door key impatiently and, as soon as she was inside, shouted her friend's name, but there was no answer.

She ran to the recreation ground, where they were still trying to extract people from the tangled heap of reinforced concrete, but no one could give her any information. Linda walked back along the road thinking disconsolately, when would this war end? It had started to rain, and then, suddenly, coming towards her out of the gloom, she saw a dishevelled Peggy. They hugged each other and Linda said,

"I thought you were dead."

"I was on my way to the shelter when it went off and I was thrown to the ground by the blast. I just got some cuts and bruises - bleeding lucky, I suppose. I've been at the First Aid Centre drinking cups of tea."

When they were back home Linda lit a fire and, when the flames were flickering in the hearth, she searched around at the back of the kitchen cupboard and produced a half bottle of whisky.

"Geoff left it behind when he was posted. I told him I don't drink the stuff and it would be there when he returned, but to hell with that - we have to celebrate; you have survived."

"What? At nine o'clock in the morning?!"

"Why not?"

She poured some whisky into two glasses, and they pulled their chairs up to the fire.

"Here's to us," Linda said, "and to victory."

They clinked glasses and each took a large gulp. Unused to strong liquor, they both coughed and spluttered then fell into fits of laughter. When they had regained their composure Peggy said, "Let's have another one."

"Yes, let's," Linda said; only this time they took a small sip.

A Railway Journey

C arlotta heaved her suitcase on to the rack and settled down in her seat amid a cacophony of slamming doors, echoing station announcements on the public address, and anxious travellers heaving luggage onto the train minutes before it was due to depart. A young soldier came into the compartment and, seeing an empty seat next to her, deposited his gear and cap and sat down, giving her a sideways glance as he did so.

He did not look more than nineteen, with regulation close-cropped hair and earnest, boyish features. She was on her way to San Diego, where she was employed as a secretary in the naval repair yards. It was three months after Pearl Harbor and the place was a hive of activity. She was from Los Angeles but, after Roosevelt's "day of infamy" speech, she moved to San Diego in order to do her bit for the war effort.

The train pulled out of the station, and an attendant came around asking if anyone would be requiring dinner. Carlotta wasn't hungry as she had already eaten, and the soldier just shook his head. He flicked through a magazine about automobiles and put it away again then, after a while, his head began to droop forward and he leaned heavily upon her.

Carlotta felt uncomfortable. Should she push him away? Wake him? She did neither and, as time passed he settled down in his seat, moving his body sideways and lowering his head until it was on her lap. She moved her legs apart to accommodate it more comfortably, and looked down upon him. He did not stir, and seemed oblivious to the intrusion on her personal space, his head nestling in the crook of her thighs as though it were a comfortable pillow.

Where did he come from, she wondered? Some mid-western hick town, in all probability. This would be an adventure for him. She looked down on his fair hair and smooth face. She guessed that he had no need to shave every day but he would, of course, lathering and scraping his stubble-less cheeks.

She was at least six years older than him, and considered herself experienced in the ways of the world, unlike this innocent who had intruded upon her. At first she held her arms stiffly by her sides but, as time passed, she felt more relaxed and cradled him in her arm. The young soldier was sleeping peacefully now and her hand, as though operating without the consent of her brain, began stroking his head. Other passengers nearby did not even look up. Perhaps they hadn't noticed them arrive separately, or maybe they assumed she was his girlfriend, or he was her younger brother. Either way, Carlotta's action did not initiate stares of disapproval. Her attitude was possessive, but she was not mothering him. On the contrary, she began to experience feelings of sexual arousal.

This is crazy, she thought; what am I doing? Common sense urged her to wake him, but she clasped him to her even more tightly and gave an audible sigh. Then, flushed with embarrassment she looked about her, but the other passengers were either reading or busy with their thoughts. Still the young man slept on, and Carlotta sat there in a state of confusion until, at last, the train juddered to a halt at the terminal.

The noise woke him and he stood up, rather self-consciously reaching for his cap and bag. He looked at her with clear blue eyes and said, "OK, babe?"

Did that mean, I'm sorry, I didn't mean to intrude, I hope you're not offended or, thanks for the loan of your lap, she wondered, but she answered, "You're welcome, soldier."

And then he was gone.

Carlotta did not hurry to leave the compartment. She could not explain what had happened, or why she had felt drawn to the young man, and needed to collect her thoughts. It was then that she noticed something shining on the floor and, picking it up, discovered it was a gold, heart-shaped pendant on a fine chain. On one side were engraved two sets of initials. The soldier must have dropped it, or perhaps it fell out of his pocket, she thought and, grabbing her case, Carlotta stepped onto the platform; but by this time he was nowhere to be seen. Back in her apartment she examined the pendant again. She presumed one set of initials were those of the soldier, and the other set those of his girlfriend; probably childhood sweethearts and close neighbours in the same small town, who went to school and grew up together, she imagined.

She struggled to remember what had been written on his kitbag; his name and number, most likely, but she had caught only a brief, partly-obscured glimpse and could recall nothing. She did not even know what unit he was in. Not knowing how to return it to its' owner, she put it in a little box containing her own few items of jewellery and, within a week, immersed as she was in her work at the repair yard, forgot all about it.

Carlotta met a naval officer called Simon Schwartz whilst working in the yards, and married him. When the war ended they went to live in Portland, Oregon, because that was where he came from. Simon returned to his civilian job as an architect, and she bore him two children. Occasionally, when they were having an evening out or meeting one of Simon's clients, she would look through her now-full jewellery box and, picking up the heart-shaped pendant, would think of the young soldier who laid his head upon her lap, and the effect his nearness had upon her.

One day Simon received a letter from a cousin of his, whom he hadn't seen since she was a small child. She was coming to Portland as part of a tour of the west coast, and could they meet?

Simon explained that on his mother's side the family came from Montana and this cousin, Emily, who was a schoolteacher and unmarried, lived in a small town in that State called Pine Creek.

Carlotta took a liking to her, although she seemed unsophisticated, and her present trip was the furthest she had travelled from home. She stayed with them for several days and, the evening before she was leaving to continue her journey, they took her out to dine in a downtown restaurant.

On a sudden impulse, because it was the first time she had ever worn it to go out, she put the heart-shaped pendant around her neck, making sure the initials were not facing outward. She had told Simon the circumstances in which she had come to acquire the pendant; that was accurate as far as it went, but some things were best left unsaid.

He looked at her with approval.

"If you like the pendant that much, I'll get a jeweller to remove the initials for you; we could even get ours engraved."

Carlotta looked shocked.

"No, that would be wrong; it would be a kind of desecration. After all, it isn't really ours to alter."

During dinner Emily kept staring at the heart-shaped pendant. Eventually she plucked up courage and said,

"That pendant reminds me of one that was given to me by a young man years ago, but when he went off to war I gave it back and said he should keep it and, if he still loved me when he came home, he could return it."

She smiled.

"The only difference is it had our initials on it."

Carlotta took it off and gave it to her husband's cousin. She examined the pendant closely, then she took out a little handkerchief and dabbed her eyes. "Emily Anne Temperley, and David Andrew Fordham," she said, looking at the initials. There was a further surprise as Emily pressed the gold heart sharply on the back, releasing a catch that opened the heart on a tiny hinge. Inside was a little photo, head and shoulders of a young man in army uniform. A tear rolled down Emily's cheek as Carlotta took the pendant from her and stared at the photo. There he was, exactly as she remembered him. For a moment she was back on that train, stroking his head as it lay on her lap. Quickly she gave it back and explained that she had sat next to the young soldier, and that she had found it under his seat after he had gone.

"I am happy to return it. I have always wanted to, but had no idea how to find the rightful owner."

Carlotta hesitated; "Men," she said, shaking her head. "I suppose he married someone else?"

"No," Emily replied, blowing her nose, "he was killed at Iwo Jima."

Mr Know-All

M r Know-All was very active in the community. He had plenty of time because he had retired early with a good pension.

His real name was Eric Stansfield-Brown.

Quite a mouthful, he would say; Call me Eric, everyone does. But that was not what they called him behind his back.

He was a town councillor and a member of the local history society. At council meetings he was always quoting precedents, and points of order. In the history society, he would correct speakers if they got the slightest detail wrong.

"I think you will find that the Dinthorp canal closed for navigation in 1898, not 1897; the last barge to pass through Dinsmere Lock was on April 3rd of that year."

To give him his due, as a councillor he was always available if anyone had a problem. These local problems usually required a simple solution; the trouble was that Stansfield-Brown didn't see it that way. He would make a mountain out of a molehill, look up ancient byelaws, hold long and largely irrelevant discussions with council officers, and write long letters to the bewildered council-tax payer, who fervently wished he had never raised the subject.

Stansfield-Brown had never married, and had no close relatives. The flat he had inherited from his deceased mother was still furnished in the post-war style, and the decoration was redolent of the fifties for the reason that nothing had been altered since that decade, even to the cracked linoleum on the floor, the original dusty drapes and the rotting net curtains on the windows. Books, correspondence, bills and other documents were scattered around the flat in no obvious order although, most of the time, he was able to locate whatever he was looking for.

There was hardly a subject on which he could not pontificate. What irritated people was the assurance with which he made his remarks - there was nothing modest or tentative about his pronouncements.

He was very proud of the fact that, as a mature student, he had obtained an arts degree from one of the newer universities, and that, of course, made him an expert on the Renaissance. On a planned holiday to Italy he studied every guide book available about the region he intended visiting, and drove the tour guide to distraction, not by asking intelligent questions, which would have been appreciated, but by his corrections, made in a tone that implied the poor guide was a half-wit. He would point out omissions, add snippets of additional information, and generally pontificate to the embarrassment of the group, who instinctively sided with their guide even if they couldn't bring themselves to tell Stansfield-Brown to shut up.

Because of his involvement in community activities he was very well-known, but this did not mean he had many friends. On the contrary, he did not have any friends, and he had never, as far as anyone knew, shown any interest in the opposite sex.

One or two people had tried to get to know him better, befriend him even, but it was hard going and, if they asked him about his early life, he just clammed up.

He also attended local adult education classes. Whatever the subject, he knew better than the tutor. He would not just present a different point of view, but argue with him or her. Worst of all, if a student asked a question he would answer it before the tutor could reply.

Then, one September, a new course started on nineteenth-century social history, a subject in which Mr Know-all had a particular interest. The tutor was new to the group, and did not know what he was letting himself in for with Eric Stansfield Brown among his students.

The first session went quietly enough, with Mr Teasdale, the tutor, introducing his subject and outlining the areas he intended to cover. He then said he liked to involve his students as much as possible, and welcomed questions and comments.

At the next few sessions Stansfield-Brown interrupted frequently, not with questions, but with statements of what he considered to be indisputable facts, made in a tone of voice that seemed to indicate that anyone disagreeing was an idiot.

Several times Mr Teasdale asked him to give others a chance to contribute, and ignored his raised hand, but this did not stop Stansfield-Brown interrupting others who were speaking or, as on previous occasions, answering questions directed at the tutor.

Then, one day, something unusual happened; the tutor lost his composure. He went red in the face, and was clearly having difficulty controlling his emotions. He looked directly at Stansfield-Brown.

"You know so much about this subject," he said, "I'm surprised you bothered to come on this course; but now that you are here and are so anxious to put everyone right, I suggest that you take over from me. Right now," he added, sitting down in a vacant seat.

To say that Stansfield-Brown was surprised would be an understatement. He looked first at Mr Teasdale and then peered short-sightedly at the whiteboard in front of the class, and then back to Teasdale again, to see if he was joking, but the tutor continued to sit with folded arms and an expressionless face.

There was a murmur in the astonished class as they waited to see what would happen next.

After what seemed an age, but was probably not more than a few minutes, Stansfield-Brown rose to his feet reluctantly and walked to the front of the class.

He did not know what to do. Of course he knew many facts about the subject under discussion, and he was particularly good with dates, but he found stringing those facts together in a coherent fashion, pointing out trends, movements and the philosophy behind them, difficult. He tried to carry on from where the tutor had left off, but what he was saying was becoming increasingly disjointed. Droplets of sweat appeared on his forehead. The class sat transfixed. His underlying insecurity was beginning to show; insecurity that he had successfully hidden for years under a cloak of bravado and brashness. Suddenly he felt very vulnerable. He moved on to a totally unrelated subject, but he had only uttered a few sentences when he came to a halt. He looked about him wild-eyed and gave a low moan. Then, without another word, he picked up his coat and, without making eye contact with anyone, walked out of the door.

The class felt uncomfortable, and rather sorry for their Mr Know-all, but Mr Teasdale continued as if nothing had happened, and Stansfield-Brown never showed his face in the class again. Not only that, he no longer turned up for History Society or council meetings. Clive, one of those colleagues at the History Society who had tried to get to know him, and who had been in the class when Stansfield-Brown walked out, decided to pay him a visit.

He found him unshaven, and wearing an old pullover with no shirt underneath. This was uncharacteristic, as he had always taken a pride in his appearance. He was reluctant to let Clive in, but eventually gave way. He seemed to have lost interest in life and just sat in an old armchair, staring vacantly at Clive.

There was no hint of the opinionated cockiness for which he was known. The flat was dirty, there was a pile of unwashed dishes in the kitchen sink and he no longer seemed to care about anything.

Clive was concerned, and asked if he had any relatives.

It turned out that Stansfield-Brown had a half-brother who was an academic, but he had fallen out with him many years ago and there was no contact.

"I'll make us some tea," Clive said, and he put the kettle on and washed out a couple of mugs.

When he was re-seated, they both sat looking at each other without saying a word. Clive knew how difficult it was for Stansfield-Brown to talk about himself, and he didn't want to pressurise him.

A few minutes passed and then, hesitantly at first, it all came out.

"I was dyslexic as a child, although it wasn't diagnosed. One teacher actually said I was stupid and wouldn't amount to anything. My birth mother died when I was young, and my step-mother was always praising her clever son by her first marriage, whilst never missing an opportunity to put me down and tell everyone how thick I was. This made me determined to succeed - I wanted to prove myself. I studied on my own and, many years after I had left school, I was accepted on a degree course. When I graduated I wrote to my brother but, instead of congratulating me, he responded by saying it was a third-rate university.

"I was so angry, and I had this intense desire to tell people how much I knew, to show off, I suppose and, well, I overdid it, didn't I?"

This was a different Mr Know-all; depressed, subdued and deflated, but suddenly with some insight.

Clive had a feeling he was going to rally.

"I'm not going back to the class," said Eric.

"Will we see you at the History Society?"

"Perhaps."

And Stansfield-Brown smiled; something he had not done for a very long time.

Retribution

C olonel James Hadow, United States Army, was sitting in his leather-upholstered swivel chair staring at a bank of computer screens. The cavernous room had the aseptic air and clinical functionality of a space-age laboratory. The Operations Centre at the Remote Warfare Defence Unit was situated an hour's drive from a small, mid-western town of no particular significance. It did have a few light industries, but most people were employed by the Army, providing support services for the base.

The Unit was situated at the foot of a mountain and was heavily guarded. The Operations Centre itself was bored out of solid rock, and accessed by a tunnel with steel doors.

There was accommodation at the base, but most married men, and that included Colonel Hadow, lived in town with their families. The colonel's daughter, Sheri, was 17 and still at school. She was pretty, and had lots of admirers but no regular boyfriend. His son, Daniel, was in his mid-twenties. He was very bright and, when a left-of-centre newspaper employed him after graduation, he began to make a name for himself as an investigative reporter. His parents were proud of his academic achievements, and the colonel had rather hoped his son would enter West Point Military Academy, and so was disappointed at his choice of career, and rather more upset that he opted for a left-wing newspaper.

"*The Gleaner* is not patriotic," he told his son. "Its aim is to run down this country and to represent us to the world in as bad a light as possible."

The topic that was on everyone's lips was the shortage of oil. The unheard of was happening; Americans were being rationed at the gas stations. This did not go down at all well with the voters, and the chances of the president being re-elected were becoming slim so, when the largest multinational signed a contract with the government of the Central Asian State of Muristan to exploit its new-found vast oil reserves, there was rejoicing all round. Except that Muristan was a small country, and the effect would be to cover nine tenths of the land with oil wells, a fact that did not bother the corrupt dictator who had ruled for many years. The installations already in place did not bode well for the future, as scant regard was paid to environmental issues. One of the attractions of Muristan for the oil company was the lack of regulation and oversight.

"A refreshing lack of red tape," was how one oil executive put it, although he added this did not mean the company would not take every precaution to avoid environmental damage.

The reality was that a once-productive agricultural land was transformed into a sea of wellheads interspersed with half-built roads, churned up mud, pools of black oil and earthworks for a giant pipeline to the west.

There was only one problem, one fly in the ointment; some of the citizens whose lands had been acquired by devious means, or for little compensation, objected to government officials and their cronies becoming multi-millionaires at the expense of the majority of the populace, who remained poor and downtrodden. They had banded together to form the Muristan Liberation Army. Their objectives were many, and sometimes conflicting, but they all agreed that a revolution was necessary if all were to benefit from the country's new-found wealth without further laying waste to their once-beautiful land. So they began by sabotaging infrastructure, and blowing up the property of some of the most corrupt officials. Warnings were given but, despite this, some people were killed.

This upset the oil executives, who had powerful friends in Washington, and the United States Secretary of State, Melvin Manson, told reporters that, whilst they would give every encouragement to Muristanis who wanted to work peacefully towards democratic institutions, violence was not the answer. The MLA was nothing more than a terrorist organisation threatening United States interests and, as such, was a legitimate target in the worldwide war on terror.

It was Friday afternoon and Daniel was on a high; not from any drugs, but from a feeling of elation at a job well done. That week he'd wrapped up an investigation on a chain of gun shops that were selling automatic weapons to anybody without even the most basic of checks; weapons that, in many cases, had been used in robberies and violent crime. The editor had congratulated him, saying that this was the kind of investigative journalism that would enhance the reputation of *The Gleaner*.

After making sure he would not be disturbed, he told Daniel that he had a special assignment for him. He was to go to Muristan, but not officially, as that would entail being embedded with American 'special advisers', and without the knowledge of CIA personnel operating in that country. He was to do this via a neighbouring country, and then make contact with the MLA to hear their side of the story. His colleagues were not to know about this in case the mission was leaked and he was prevented from carrying out this objective.

Two weeks later Daniel was in Muristan. He had entered the country illegally via a neighbouring state, having crossed the border with the help of a tribesman whom he paid in dollars.

The same man set up a meeting with a MLA sympathiser, who was very suspicious when he realised he was an American, but Daniel managed to convince the man that he was an independent journalist and so he agreed to try and arrange a meeting with one of the leaders of the movement.

First he was taken to a safe house, little more than a wood-and-corrugated-iron shack in a makeshift encampment at the bottom of a stony hillside. Men sat around in sad groups, and undernourished children played in the dirt.

"Who are these people?" he asked his companion. "Why are they here in this barren place?"

"They are landless farmers, forced to move from land now covered with oil wells."

"Surely they received compensation"?

"The government says that they did, but they were forced to make their claims through government-appointed lawyers, who undervalued their land and siphoned off most of the compensation in fees and expenses."

"I would like to interview one of them; would you interpret for me?"

"I'm afraid I can't, as I have to go now, but I will be back tomorrow. These people know you are here, and will bring you some food tonight. The sleeping arrangements are basic, but it's the best I can do."

The food, when it came, was simple but adequate. He felt guilty taking food from people with so little. He spent a restless night fully-clothed on a rough mattress and, the next morning, washed in a stream a hundred yards from the shack. Although still very early, it wasn't long before his nameless companion drove up in a battered pick-up, leaving a cloud of dust.

"Come," he said, "Let us hope we are not stopped; it will be difficult to explain your presence."

They drove through an industrial landscape of oil wells, pools of black oil where spills had occurred, and half-completed infrastructure. Suddenly the pick-up slithered to a halt.

"I have to blindfold you now, and you must give me your word that you will not remove it until you are told; otherwise, no interview."

Daniel agreed and, an hour later, the pick-up stopped again, and this time he was helped out of the vehicle still blindfolded, and ushered into a building and down some steps into a basement room, where his blindfold was removed.

There were two men in the windowless room; one was standing near the door with a gun at his belt. He searched Daniel, but allowed him to keep the three items in his possession; his wallet, his passport and a Smartphone. While replacing the phone, he had surreptitiously opened a line to a special phone at the office of *The Gleaner*, where everything said was being recorded. The other man, who was wearing army-style fatigues and had a bushy beard, was seated at a table. He motioned Daniel to sit down at the only other chair in the room.

"What do you want?" he said brusquely.

Daniel explained that he'd heard the State Department's and the majority US media's view that the MLA were terrorists doing their best to sabotage their country's economy and future, but he worked for an independent newspaper, which wanted to hear and print a view of the situation from the Muristan Liberation Army's perspective. Then he asked who the bearded man was.

"I am currently in charge of our operations; that is all you need to know. A gang of crooks runs this country, and the biggest crook of all is our president. They are all totally corrupt; he appoints his friends as ministers, and they are unashamedly filling their pockets at the expense of the ordinary citizen and, to cap it all, they are desecrating this fair country of ours."

He spoke clearly, in good English.

"All other methods have failed; many of those who protested have disappeared, so we have no other choice except to blow up their installations. It is not our objective to kill people, although there have been a few unfortunate accidents."

He was about to continue when the door burst open and a man shouted something in Muristani.

"We must leave immediately," the bearded man said, rising. "Follow me and run for your life - a drone is approaching."

Daniel didn't hesitate. Sticking close behind, he was up the stairs and out of the building in less than a minute. Several other men and a woman were all running in different directions; then there was an almighty explosion.

Colonel James Hadow studied his screen. The CIA had identified a Muristan Liberation Army base that housed one of the terrorist's commanders, and had passed on the coordinates to the Remote Warfare Operations Centre. A drone had taken off from a base many miles away, and Hadow could see it approaching the target area. Remotely swivelling the on-board camera, he could see the isolated building dead ahead.

He did not hesitate before pressing the key that would release the missile and guide it directly to its target. These were the bad guys, blowing things up, preventing progress. The camera showed some people running, and then the scene was obliterated.

The Gleaner's editor listened to the recording from Daniel's phone. It was all there; the shout of alarm, the noise of running and then, abruptly, the phone went dead. Later that day, *Fox News* announced that that there had been a successful drone-strike on the terrorists' base, and that a senior MLA commander had been killed.

The next day, *The Gleaner* put out a special edition. The paper questioned the US government's policy, and portrayed Daniel as a courageous journalist. The editor also managed to get himself interviewed on countrywide television.

The first Colonel Hadow knew that he had been responsible for his son's death was when his wife, Madge, came running out of the house screaming incoherently about Daniel. He stopped tying up the rose bush and held her.

"For God's sake, Madge, what is it?"

"It's Daniel; it's been on the news; he's been killed by one of your drones," she sobbed.

The Colonel couldn't believe what he was hearing; it didn't make sense, there must be some mistake.

"It's true; he went to talk to those people, to find out why…"

Overwhelmed, she couldn't continue, and he went to console her but she pushed him away with a force that surprised him.

He stood there in the garden looking at his wife, numb and uncomprehending.

Could That Have Been Me?

The headline in the evening paper caught my eye. *14-YEAR-OLD CHARGED WITH RAPE*, it screamed. I bought a copy and read further. *A fourteen-year-old boy, who cannot be named for legal reasons, has been charged with raping a 15-year-old girl. The police spokeswoman said she could make no further comment except to say that the boy would be appearing in the Magistrates' Court the following morning.*

My eyes refocused on the headline, and I could see nothing but the bold black letters. The words "14-year-old" and "rape" flashed before me and reawakened memories that had been long buried and forgotten.

It took me back to 1944, to a picturesque market town in Yorkshire perched above a river that flowed at the bottom of a steep valley. I was 14 and lived with my mother and two younger brothers in a requisitioned house that we shared with another family, a mother and daughter who, like us, were taking refuge from the flying bombs that were raining down on London. One other thing we had in common was that both my dad and five-year-old Annie's dad were away in the Army.

For me it was the time of adolescence, of confused emotions. Exciting, new and, at times, guilt-ridden. In those days they didn't have sex education, and what information we had was picked up from our peers. My mum had tried to help. She gave me a book to read which explained what you had to do, but the book said that you had to be in love first, and married, and it left a lot of questions unanswered.

I went to the local school, and I joined the youth club. The club leader was a musically-gifted and rather effeminate man, whose abiding passion was producing musical shows. Boys and girls showing the slightest degree of talent were enrolled into the cast of whatever he was currently directing. Consequently, most evenings were taken up with rehearsals, and those not engaged in this activity were left to their own devices, which usually meant playing table tennis or just hanging around.

The sexes tended to stay in their own small groups, although there was some intermingling and a lot of banter that we thought clever and amusing. I had attached myself to a group of three boys who went around together. There was Johnny, known as "Jelly" Johnson, who told jokes, and was a mine of information about sexual matters new to us. There was Bob Harding, not yet 15 but six feet tall, and Albert Jopling, known as Joppo, who had a laugh like a horse neighing; and then there was me, Tom Grainger.

There was a girl at the club called Ellen, who was 15 and worked as a shop assistant in the market square. She had a bit of a reputation because she always had an answer and gave as good as she got when boys whistled, or made remarks about her. She was always going home with different boys. They were never invited inside but would stand outside the front door, which was down a side alley, kissing for what seemed ages. I know because, if it were Jelly or Bob taking her home, they wanted me to tag along and wait for them at the end of the alley. If they groped a bit too much, she would say,

"Give over, I've got to go in now," and sometimes her mum would lean out of a window and say,

"Come on, girl, it's time you were in."

One night I got to take her home by myself. There had been a social at the club and, after joining in the Gay Gordons and the Hokey-Cokey, I found myself dancing the last waltz with her. After I had trodden on her toes several times, she asked me if we could go. As we drew near to her house, I became tongue-tied and couldn't think of anything to say. When we reached her front door I said, "See you at the club," and, before she had a chance to reply, gave the surprised Ellen a quick kiss, and ran as though my life depended on it. I was mad at myself for being so shy; I had wanted to be confident, to make her laugh, and to give the impression that taking girls home and kissing them was a regular occurrence. She would never look at me again or, if she did, it would be to point me out to her friends and make fun of me.

A few days later I met up with Jelly and the others.

"We saw you go off with Ellen. Go on - tell us what happened," he sniggered. "We're dying to know."

I said nothing, but my face went a shade of red, and they all laughed. We had been dawdling along the road, and we stopped outside *The Feathers*, the pub run by Bob's parents. It was four o'clock, and the bar was shut.

"Why don't you come inside? Me mam and dad are out," he said slyly.

We sat in the Public Bar whilst Bob half-filled pint glasses with bitter and topped them up with lemonade.

"Get them down you," he smirked. "Me dad won't know if we wash up glasses."

Joppo got out some *Woodbines* and handed them around. The conversation returned to Ellen, and Jelly was not going to let me off the hook.

"How far did you get with her?" he demanded.

Feeling cornered, I said, "Not very far. Her mum must have seen us because she told her to go indoors straight away."

They fell about laughing. If they were to be believed I was the only one of them who hadn't actually had his hands inside Ellen's knickers. They all agreed that she would egg them on, and then, when she decided they had gone far enough, would say, "Leave off," or "Give over now."

"She's a right little teaser," Bob said.

Jelly looked conspiratorial.

"Know what I think? I think she's asking for it. Why else would she hang around with us lot knowing that we don't leave school 'til next month, and her already out earning money?"

"It's a well-known fact," said Joppo. "When they lead you on like that, they really want it, even when they say no."

Jelly agreed.

"Why don't we get her alone somewhere and have a bit of fun with her?"

"Yeah, why don't we?" said Joppo, and gave one of his silly laughs.

"Ellen is not that stupid," I said, "She'll get hopping mad."

"She might play hard to get, but when she sees we're not takin' no for an answer, she'll do what we want right enough," Jelly replied.

Joppo butted in. "When we going t' do it, then?"

"We'll get her down by the river," Jelly said. "She usually takes her dog down there on a Sunday morning."

Bob glanced at the bar clock.

"Look at time. Gaffers 'll be home soon. We'll have to go."

They all wandered down to the market square and stood outside the chemist shop where Ellen worked. Jelly said he wanted some cough sweets and so we all went inside. It was the first time I had seen Ellen since the night of the social, and my heart pumped a little faster.

"What are you doing here?" she said to Jelly. "Go away."

"I'll have some of those cough sweets."

"That doesn't take four of you."

"Will you be going down by the river on Sunday?"

"That'll be sixpence ha'penny. I might do; what do you want to know for?"

"It's your birthday next week, isn't it?"

"Yes, it is. What's it to you, Johnny Johnson?"

We've got something for you," he lied; "We're going to give it to you on Sunday morning, by the river."

Ellen looked surprised, but a customer anxious to be served distracted her attention. Old Linklater, the owner, was hovering in the background, and was none too pleased at the presence of four youths whose contribution to his turnover was negligible.

"Be on your way, lads," he said, with barely concealed hostility and, as we departed, Jelly shouted across the shop,

"See you on Sunday then, Ellen."

On Sunday morning we met up, and walked down by the river. We waited near a small copse of elms that bordered the path. As we hung about we discussed what we would do when she showed up. Jelly said we should persuade her to go into the copse where we could not be seen.

I felt apprehensive. Were we really about to do something I knew to be wrong? Then, as they conspired, I became scared and wished I had no part in their scheme.

The morning wore on, and there was no sign of Ellen.

"She'll come," said Jelly; "She always walks her puppy along the river path; regular as clockwork."

We started skimming flat stones over the surface of the river to see who could make them bounce the most, but still no Ellen. We had fantasised, and worked ourselves up to commit this crime, but could not sustain this for an indefinite period. The plain fact was we were beginning to get bored. Time passed, and suddenly Bob said he'd better be going home for his dinner. Slowly, we made our excuses and drifted off.

What would have happened if Ellen had taken her puppy for a walk by the river that morning? Perhaps nothing, it was probably boyish bravado. Anyway, Ellen could stand up for herself and, if we had threatened her, she would have wiped the floor with us, told us exactly where to get off, wouldn't she? But would that have stopped Jelly and, if not, what would have been the consequences?

I looked at the newspaper headline once again. **Could that have been me**?

Bob Briscoe's Dream Girl

Bob Briscoe was a retired electronics engineer. Still in his sixties, he missed his colleagues and the opportunities for socialising afforded by his employment, because he had very few other friends. His wife was not in good health; in fact, following an accident some years previously she could no longer climb stairs. He had suggested installing a stair lift, but she maintained this would not solve the problem because she couldn't get in and out of the bath. They already had a downstairs shower, and a spare room originally intended as a dining room, so she said she would sleep downstairs. He did not object to this arrangement, because she had long since lost interest in the physical side of their relationship.

Bob had been a rather shy person as a young man, and had not had any affairs prior to his marriage and, now that he was retired, he began to feel that he had missed out, and was prone to fantasising about imaginary relationships.

His main consolation and hobby – electronic experimentation – was really just a continuation of his working life, only now he was free to choose those areas that interested him. He had converted one of the upstairs rooms into a lab, in which he spent much of his day amid a jumble of computer hardware and electronic gadgetry.

His wife complained that he was always ordering expensive items of equipment, but whenever she wanted something new for the house it was like getting blood out of a stone. Since his retirement he had been experimenting with lasers in an attempt to produce a holographic moving image directly from his computer monitor. To this end he had spent many hours of original research in a fruitless effort to achieve his goal. His guilty secret was the web address he was using for these experiments - one where, for a fee, a lady with a webcam would disrobe and pose for him.

One day when this young lady was on his monitor, he connected up his apparatus and focused his lasers at a spot in the centre of the lab. Nothing happened at first and then, after he had made some further adjustments, a hologram appeared in the centre of the floor. To his immense pride he had at last succeeded, and he watched with pleasure as the shadowy figure moved in unison with the image on the screen.

Then something very strange happened, and he had to look twice to make sure his senses were not deceiving him. The two scantily-clad images were not doing the same thing. Furthermore, the hologram began to seem more real, more lifelike than ever. Instinctively he put out his hand, and recoiled in horror; he had felt solid flesh!

The hologram smiled.

"Yes," she said, "I am quite firm," and she stepped out of the beam of light.

Bob opened his mouth to speak, but no words came out.

"Do you like me?" the hologram said, twirling around.

"I…you…how did you get here?" He needed an explanation.

"You may well ask. It was you who brought me here."

Bob looked again at the image on the monitor and quickly back to the young woman, who was still there in front of him. Regaining some of his composure, he pointed at the screen.

"Her name was - is Sharon; is that yours?"

"Yes."

"But you are not her, so who, or what are you; a double, a spirit, a *doppelganger*?"

"I am all of those."

Suddenly Bob thought about his wife, who was sitting reading downstairs.

"Are you permanent?" he said, beginning to get anxious.

"No, of course not. As soon as you close the tab I will disappear."

She moved closer to him.

"You haven't answered my question."

"What question was that?"

"I said: do you like me?"

"Yes, of course; you're very attractive."

"Well then, are you just going to stand there and gaze at me?"

She looked at him with an amused smile.

He couldn't believe it, but he led her into the adjoining bedroom. They were there for some time, but all good things come to an end and eventually they returned to the lab. She stepped back into the laser beam and, when he closed the link, she promptly disappeared.

Afterwards, there was nothing to suggest that she had ever been there except, Bob thought, a faint scent of perfume.

His wife, who was slightly deaf, had heard nothing but, later that day after they had eaten their evening meal, he became aware that she was staring at him.

"What's the matter? Something wrong?" he said.

"No, nothing. I was just thinking you're looking very pleased with yourself today. If I didn't know any better, I'd say you'd just had a large win on the horses."

"Some chance of that!"

"No chance, I'd say. You would rather spend your money on your precious equipment than risk a flutter."

During the next few weeks he repeated the procedure, Sharon materialising in front of him and stepping out of the hologram. He felt sure his wife would hear something, but she had the volume of the TV set high and was blissfully unaware of what was going on.

She did, however, notice a change in his personality. He became more attentive to her and more cheerful. He remembered their anniversary and told her he had booked a table in a local restaurant. She was dumbfounded, as treats like that were rare occurrences. She wondered what had brought about this transformation, but didn't ask him. It was enough that he was more considerate, and she wasn't one for enquiring into people's motivations, even if the person was her husband.

Bob looked forward to his rendezvous with Sharon, as she was a compliant and accommodating spectre.

One day, they were together when Bob became aware of an intense pain in his chest, and he could not breathe. Even Bob's wife heard the crash and wondered momentarily if anything was wrong, but she was used to strange noises emanating from above and did not become worried until he failed to come downstairs at his usual time. She called out, and tried to climb the stairs, but found it beyond her. She had no alternative but to dial 999 and explain her predicament. During the twenty minutes it took for the ambulance to arrive, she sat at the bottom of the stairs and periodically called out, "Bob; are you all right?" but there was no response.

The two paramedics went straight upstairs, carrying their equipment with them. The laboratory was in a mess, with everything lying jumbled up on the bench and the floor. From the landing another open door led off to the main bedroom, and in there they found Bob's naked and inert figure lying on the bed. He was beyond resuscitation. They had seen death many times and were not upset by it, but they were surprised by what lay partially obscured by his body and was fully revealed when they turned him over. It was a life-sized doll, exquisitely detailed, with real chestnut hair, and anatomically perfect in every respect.

As they lifted him off the bed, the doll's legs flopped open. There was a slight click, and a softly seductive voice said, "Hello sweetie."

Princess Zaza

S he hated these Northern towns, but then she hated London. The succession of boarding houses and rented rooms, her possessions, such as they were, carted around from place to place. She had no roots, but that was her life.

At least in London she could remain anonymous, and that suited her. The downside was that you could be lying sick in your room for a week and no one would give a fig. But in this place she knew that everyone would want to know her business.

The taxi drew up at the address that Lydia had been given, and the driver deposited her suitcase and a holdall on the pavement.

A middle-aged woman with cracked, red fingernails and a dress that was too tight for a figure that was past its prime opened the door.

"Are you Mrs Jobson?"

"Yes."

"I was given your name by a friend."

She was not a friend, but that did not matter.

"I'd like a room," Lydia said.

"How long for?"

"Just for the week."

"Oh." The woman looked disappointed.

"Will you be requiring food?"

"Yes."

"An evening meal?"

"Yes, but I won't be in till late."

She eyed Lydia curiously.

"In that case it will have to be a cold plate. Come in and I will show you to your room."

She made no attempt to help Lydia with her bags. The house smelled of boiled cabbage, old horsehair sofas and mouse droppings. The room was cold and drab, but had the essentials.

"What's the purpose of your visit?" the landlady asked.

Lydia had been expecting this.

"I'm helping out at *Finnegan's*."

Finnegan's had started life as a music hall, but had deteriorated into a second-rate variety theatre.

The landlady was not satisfied; what did she mean, "helping out"? She looked at Lydia's plain, rather dowdy dress, and face free of make-up, and said sarcastically,

"The theatricals usually stay at Mrs Lambert's in North Street."

Lydia did not answer, and Mrs Jobson left her to unpack.

She wasn't due at *Finnegan's* until later that day, and so Mrs Jobson gave her some lunch. The landlady said she had other boarders.

"Of course, they are not here during the day; they're business people."

What sort of business people would choose to live here, she wondered?

A young man walked into the room; mid-twenties, Lydia thought. He had greasy skin and spots, like an adolescent. He wore a sports jacket, a pale shirt and a tie with visible food stains. He looked briefly at Lydia and turned to Mrs Jobson.

"I'm off out, Mum."

"Don't be late back, Martin," she called after him, "I'm cooking your favourite tonight."

After lunch Lydia came downstairs with her bulky holdall and, using the hall telephone, phoned for a taxi.

At *Finnegan's*, the show's producer and theatre-owner looked Lydia up and down in disbelief.

"You're not Princess Zaza, exotic dancer; the one who sent me the photos?"

"Yes I am," she said crossly. "You don't expect me to look the part when I'm not on stage, do you?"

"Well, no, Miss Dean," he said, taking one of her photos out of a file and looking at it again.

"We shall have to see how the audience react tonight, won't we"?

"Yes," Lydia said, "Now, can I meet the band leader? I have to discuss my act with him."

The band leader and conductor, a jaded individual who had seen some pretty bad acts in his time, humoured her as she told him what music she wanted to accompany her routine.

"I don't want any of your stock tunes," she said, handing out sheet music, "and I shall want all these back at the end of the week."

The bandleader looked at the music in surprise; it included an excerpt from Shahrazad.

Lydia was lucky in that she had a small cubby-hole of a dressing room to herself, and Lew Bridges, the owner-producer, made it clear that he was doing her a big favour that he hoped he wouldn't regret.

She sat down quietly and looked at herself in the mirror without moving for five minutes. She knew she was going to change, not just her physical appearance, but also her personality. She took off her loose-fitting, frumpy clothes, exposing the full-breasted, shapely figure that she carefully hid from the world when she wasn't performing, and put on a revealing stage costume. Then she loosened and rearranged her hair, and applied make-up. Finally, she added false eyelashes and some costume jewellery that transformed her into the exotic, fantasy creature that was her stage presence.

She was given a call to say she was on next, and went to the wings, where she did some stretches to warm up while waiting for the mime artist who preceded her to finish his act that was accompanied only by music and sound effects. He looked alternately sad and happy, puzzled and amused as he reacted to everyday situations, but he made the audience laugh, and she was impressed with the skill of his performance.

He side-stepped to avoid Lydia and then bowed comically at her as he came off. His action made her smile, and relaxed her as she made her entrance. She posed for a second before lifting a shapely leg, and began dancing to an oriental melody. Then the tempo changed. She twirled, she shook, she shimmied, her lithe body twisted and turned sensually and suggestively as she danced to popular tunes. A spotlight reflecting on sequins sent out dazzling flashes of light and colour. The dance style changed again; her choice was eclectic but effective, and the audience loved it. Then, the music still playing, she descended the steps and danced along the front row, dodging outstretched hands trying to touch her. It was then that she noticed Mrs Jobson's son, Martin, sitting in the front row. Did he recognise her, she wondered, as she returned to the stage for her finale amid whistles and applause? Lew, the producer, who had watched her performance, said she could extend her act for a further week, but Lydia declined, saying she had other commitments.

After she had changed and was about to leave, there was a knock on the door and a cheerful, good-looking man, elegantly dressed, squeezed into the tiny dressing-room.

Lydia did not encourage fans; she did not know this man and was about to tell him to leave, when he said,

"Let me introduce myself. I am Masonovitch the Mime, but you can call me Boris. I was impressed with your dancing; your fluidity and your ability to move effortlessly from one genre to another were quite superb."

Lydia looked at him in amazement. Was this the sad, white-faced loser, part Chaplin and part Marcel Marceau, who acrobatically performed as if the empty stage were full of tables, chairs, cupboards, and impedimenta of all kinds?

"Thank you," she said. "My name is Lydia. I didn't recognize you at first. You look so different from that sad, accident-prone figure."

He looked at her plain dress and beige woolly cardigan.

"You look pretty different yourself; not at all like the sensual show-off I saw on stage," he said, smiling.

She flushed.

"That's my alter ego; I'm really a very private person."

"Would you like to have dinner with me this evening? I can vouch for the food."

Without giving it any thought she said,

"No thank you, my landlady has prepared something."

"Perhaps another time," he said, as he bade her goodnight.

She didn't see Mrs Jobson when she returned, because she had her own private sitting-room that was sacrosanct but, when she saw what had been left for her, some fatty ham and tired-looking salad, she wished that she had accepted his invitation, especially after a fly settled on the uncovered plate. She was about to go to her room when she heard the front door slam and Martin walked in.

"You're a sly one," he said, smirking, "Hiding your light, or should I say your assets, from us all. Wait till I tell Mother."

She watched him eyeing her up and down with a silly smile on his face.

"I'd rather you didn't because, if you do, I shall have to find somewhere else to stay. I like to keep my private life completely separate from my stage performance."

He came closer and she could smell his odour, a combination of sweat and beer.

"Well, it could be our secret," he said, with a sly grin. "My room is just across the landing from yours," and he put his arm out as if he were going to touch her, but changed his mind when she drew back. That night, when she went to bed, she locked her door.

She slept late, and what she wanted more than anything when she woke was a shower, but her room had only a washbasin. There, she knew, a bathroom along the corridor, so putting on a housecoat she padded along the corridor to the bathroom. No shower, but a large bath. The door had a small bolt on it, and this she closed before running some water that was just warm. It was not a bath to luxuriate in so she quickly washed, and was about to step out when the door opened and Martin walked in. He stood there looking at her, with that silly smile of his, as Lydia grabbed a towel to wrap around her.

"The door was open," he said.

"It wasn't; or at least it wouldn't have been if anything in this place worked." She was angry. "Now please leave."

She knew then that she would have to find somewhere else to stay for the rest of her engagement.

The next day at *Finnegan's* was a matinee. This house was rarely full, and was mostly attended by pensioners, but it gave Lydia the opportunity to leave the house early. Mrs Jobson was none too pleased when she came down with her bag packed.

"I'm afraid I can't give you a refund, as you booked the room for the week," she said crossly.

Lydia did not argue; she was glad to get away from this depressing place.

At the theatre she spoke to the mime artist.

"Do you know if Mrs Lambert has any vacancies?"

"Mrs who?"

"The theatrical landlady."

"I wouldn't know, Lydia; I'm not staying there. What's the problem"?

She explained that her accommodation until this morning was dirty and depressing and, to cap it all, she was plagued by the landlady's lecherous son.

"I'm staying at the *White Hart Hotel*," he said, "and I'm sure they will have room there."

"Won't that be rather expensive?"

His face creased into a big smile.

"Well, in the ordinary way perhaps, but my brother happens to be the manager and I am sure, as a favour to me, he will quote you reasonable terms."

After the evening performance Boris took Lydia back to the *White Hart* and secured her a room. It was clean and bright, and bore no comparison to Mrs Jobson's depressing accommodation.

"And now let me buy you dinner," he said.

Lydia was very independent-minded and normally would have insisted on going Dutch but, on this occasion, she didn't. Later, she pondered on why she had broken her rule but could not come to any firm conclusion.

The next day they watched each other's performance from the wings, but it was their off-stage persona that they both found appealing.

He liked the fact she did not draw attention to herself, and that off-stage she was modest but, being perceptive, he could see that despite these efforts there was an innate sensuality about her that manifested itself in little more than a subtle look, or in the way she moved.

The next night they dined together again, and the next day they spent time together before, after and between performances. Other artistes nudged each other or gave a wink. Lydia, whose past experiences had made her wary of men, felt comfortable and reassured in Boris's company.

She knew that his jovial, outgoing manner hid a more sensitive, whimsical side to his personality. They talked easily, smiled a lot, and she spent time in his room. On the last night of the engagement at *Finnegan's*, she never left it.

The next day they were to go their separate ways, he to a booking in Belgium, she to an end of pier on the south coast.

"Is this the end for us?" she said sadly.

"No, Lydia, we will remain friends and keep in touch."

"Friends; is that all?"

He hesitated.

"I have commitments."

"And so do I," she said.

At the train station they said their last goodbyes. His train came in first but, just as he was about to board, a thought struck her.

"Boris," she cried, "Don't board this train; there will be another; I have an idea!"

He hesitated for a moment before letting the train depart, and they went into the station café.

"Well?" he said, when they were settled.

"We admire each other's performance, right?"

"Right."

"Then why don't we plan a joint act?"

He was about to speak, but she put her hand on his arm.

"Listen, it's not as crazy as it sounds. In your act you fall for a flickering image on a screen. What if you fell in love with a real dancer, someone who was too grand to even look twice at you? There would be real pathos in that; the audience would love it."

He did not answer immediately and she waited, heart pounding.

"It's a good idea," he said at last, "And I think it would work. But before we go any further, it's time I told you something about myself;

I'm gay."

She looked perplexed. "But what about last night?"

"I'm very sorry; I did not want to disappoint you."

"That changes things," she said sadly, "I thought…"

"I know what you thought, and I should not have encouraged you, but I do like and admire you, so let's keep in touch."

Lydia sighed, "Yes, let's."

A Fateful Meeting

T he discovery of the emails on his wife's computer was the last straw. Dave Goodman had arrived home late, having crossed the Channel in a desperate effort to drum up new business. The situation was hopeless for, although his wife Jean did not know it, he was broke, up to his eyes in debt. The firm he started eight years ago to sell trimmings to the fashion industry was finished. His biggest customers had found other, cheaper sources of supply. It was largely due to Jean's extravagant lifestyle and her constant demands for money that had caused him to price himself out of the market. Not without apprehension, he had planned to break the news to his wife that very evening, but she was not at home. She had left a message suggesting that he microwave a ready meal from the freezer, but giving no indication as to where she had gone.

On previous occasions when she had done this Jean had mentioned the name of a woman friend, and so Dave wondered whether she had received an email from someone that morning causing her to change her plans. He opened her Inbox, but the only communication was dated two days earlier, and so he looked in the Deleted Items folder and found a lot of emails from someone named Drew, and they were mostly of an explicitly sexual nature. The one dated that day said that he was desperate to see Jean, and could they meet that very evening? Her reply, found in Sent Items, was equally enthusiastic, and left nothing to the imagination about what they intended doing when they met.

When Dave had taken this in, he sat thinking for a while in semi-darkness, feeling utterly depressed. The future looked black and he felt that he had nothing to live for. Then he made a decision - he would end it all, leave her to sort out all his debts. Perhaps her lover would help, or perhaps his ardour for Jean would suddenly diminish when he found out what financial straits she was in; but how to end his life? He didn't want to take an overdose and for her to find him dead or, worse still, alive but gravely ill. No, he would go away to a remote place, a Scottish mountainside for example, take a few sleeping tablets and die peacefully of hypothermia. She would report him missing and, a week or two later, his body would be found by a walker. He wasn't sure how he was going to get to his destination or, indeed, where it was, but as a first step he phoned for a taxi to take him to Paddington, from where he travelled on the underground to King's Cross. If the taxi driver happened to remember him, the police would think he was going to the West Country.

Although it was late, as luck would have it the last train that day was leaving for Edinburgh. It was not crowded, because it arrived at its destination at some unearthly hour, but in his present state of mind this was of no consequence. He found a window seat in the coach furthest from the barrier and closed his eyes. Shortly before the train left the station, someone walked up the aisle and sat down in the seat facing him. Dave cursed inwardly; he did not feel sociable, and he kept his eyes shut. Within minutes the train was through the northern suburbs and was speeding towards Peterborough.

He opened his eyes and stared, blankly at first, at the man opposite him, who was reading. As his eyes became more focused, he began to study this fellow-passenger. He was the same build as Dave, probably the same height and, like Dave, he had protruding ears. Come to think of it, his hair was the same colour, although shorter, and his nose was the same shape. He suddenly became interested; how curious - the man was his double.

The other passenger lowered his book.

"Are you thinking what I'm thinking?" he said, smiling.

"If you had your hair cut shorter, I don't think anyone could tell us apart."

Dave agreed, and said it was a strange coincidence, and then he lapsed into silence.

"Short business trip?" the stranger enquired.

He had already noted that Dave had no luggage in the rack.

Dave said, "No," and then regretted it, because his answer roused the other man's curiosity.

"Well, you are obviously not going on holiday…"

Dave didn't reply.

"Look," the man said, "I don't mean to pry, but I am intrigued."

He studied Dave for a moment.

"I'm going to trust you, and tell you something about myself, and then perhaps you will reciprocate; but first, you must promise that what I say will go no further."

Dave promised. What difference did it make? He'd be dead within a few days.

"My name is Ted, Ted Howard. I have a successful Internet business selling prints and original paintings online. I am divorced and live on my own in a comfortable apartment, but for some years have been bored out of my mind, and have been planning to start a completely new life in Chile. I have transferred a substantial sum of money into an offshore account, and I plan to disappear and never return. I have on me a letter to my solicitor that I will post tomorrow, instructing him to wind-up my affairs and deposit the resulting capital sum in a numbered Swiss account, leaving him with no knowledge of my whereabouts. The letter will be postmarked Edinburgh, and tomorrow I will fly on the shuttle to Heathrow to catch my flight."Dave looked at him in amazement.

"Why on earth do you want to do that? Unlike me, you have everything going for you; it doesn't make sense."

"It makes sense to me! Now tell me, why are you going to Edinburgh without so much as a briefcase?"

"I'm not going to Edinburgh specifically; it's just the first stage of a one-way journey."

"One way?"

"Just as you asked me to respect your confidence, now I will have to ask you to do the same."

"Your story is safe with me. I shall soon be thousands of miles away, so why should I care what you are going to do?"

Dave introduced himself and told his fellow passenger about his bankrupt business and his wife's infidelity. He said he was also running away, but there would be no happy ending, as he planned to end his life.

They were both silent for a while as each of them considered the other's confession; then Ted looked about him to see if anyone had come within earshot, but their end of the carriage was deserted.

"I've been thinking," he said; "I want to change my identity and disappear, and you - you want to be a martyr; but is that necessary? If you could change *your* identity, and had the means to start a new life, leaving your unfaithful wife to deal with the financial mess you left behind, wouldn't that be preferable?"

"Wishful thinking; I'm broke!"

Ted leaned forward.

"I have an idea," he said. "Why don't we swap identities? If you were to have a haircut, no one could tell us apart. I tear up my letter and you return to

London, live in my flat and run my business as if you were me. I, on the other hand, disappear as you."

"That's a fanciful scheme, but I don't get it - what's in it for you?"

"Don't you see? Nobody will know that I have disappeared, and I will be able to lead a new life without anyone suspecting the truth."

"Yes, but you lose the capital from the sale of your apartment and business."

"As I said, I have made adequate provision for my future but, if you have a conscience about it, you could always make regular payments into my Swiss account, although it would have to be done in a way that would not show up on the balance sheet."

Dave looked out of the window into the inky blackness. All he could see was Ted's reflection.

"I am trying to take this in," he said. "It can't be that easy; there are bound to be problems. What do I know about your business?"

"Nothing to it, I'm just a retailer. I don't buy and sell old masters. Artists bring me their paintings, and I take them on a commission basis if I think they will sell. Customers view them on the website. You'll soon get the hang of it! Well, tell me; are you game for it?"

Dave was silent for a moment, and then he said,

"Yes, I am; what have I got to lose?"

And they shook hands across the table. Ted's mind had been racing ahead ever since Dave had confided in him.

"This is what we do," he said.

"We spend the rest of this journey practising each other's signature. We swap credit cards and pin numbers, and when we get to Edinburgh I book a twin-bedded room in a good hotel in your name. Don't worry, I won't use your card, I'll pay for two nights' bed and breakfast in advance with cash. "I'm afraid you will have to hang around until the shops open, when you can get yourself a haircut so that we look exactly the same. I will phone you on your mobile to tell you the room number, so that you can come up without arousing suspicion; then you can hand your phone over for me to dispose of. Reception must think there is only one of us in the room – I'll say I slept in the second bed because the first one wasn't comfortable. We will need the few days together so that I can fill you in with details of my business and way of life. Damn, I have just thought of a snag; I will need your passport."

"Don't worry, that's not a problem. I was in Calais this morning," Dave looked at his watch, "or rather yesterday morning, and I still have it on me."

He followed Ted's instructions to the letter. He had his hair cut and, as he walked to a nearby café he felt very tired, but considerably more cheerful than when he started his journey. While sipping coffee, Dave turned on his mobile phone; there were two messages, one from his wife asking where he had gone and would he phone her as soon as possible, and the other from Ted, giving him details of the hotel and room number.

Ted answered his knock.

"You look dead beat; you may as well have a sleep, we can talk later," he said.

Dave slept soundly for several hours, and woke to find Ted sitting in the armchair studying him with a thoughtful expression. They put a "Do not disturb" notice on the door and spent the afternoon giving each other the information they would need to change places; then, at six o'clock, Ted said he was going out for something to eat. He would be gone about an hour, and when he returned it would be Dave's turn to go out.

Dave watched television to pass the time and when, after an hour and a half, Ted had not returned, he became concerned. Shortly afterwards he decided to investigate, and he slipped past the receptionist and into the street while her back was turned. The road ahead of him was blocked, and a small crowd had formed. As he drew near he could see a man lying in the road, with several people bending over him. A vehicle was parked awkwardly, its front wheels up on the pavement, and the driver, obviously distressed, was standing by the open door saying to anyone who would listen,

"He came out of nowhere. Suddenly he was in front of me and there was nothing I could do!"

Dave went over to the prone figure and, to his horror, realised that it was Ted. Blood oozed from a massive head wound. The man next to him was looking at the ground.

"He's dead," he said, without glancing at Dave, and then the wail of sirens could be heard as a police car and ambulance came racing to the scene. Dave moved away quickly, his mind in a turmoil; what should he do now? He found a café and sat down to think. Ted had Dave's ID, so the police and his wife would think him dead. There was nothing to stop him proceeding with Ted's plan, and returning to London as Ted. Using Ted's debit card, he drew some money out of his account and purchased a ticket back to King's Cross.

Dave unlocked the door to Ted's apartment with a feeling of unreality. It was, as the estate agents say, well-appointed. This was not some pokey bachelor pad, but a comfortable home. The second bedroom was a good size, and had been converted into a well-equipped office, with the latest model computer and racks containing many pictures. The walls were bare, except for one small picture that seemed familiar to him. Was it a print? He took it off the wall to have a closer look, and found a wall-safe behind it with a combination lock. Strange, Ted had been very thorough, but the one thing that had slipped his mind was the combination for the safe. Perhaps he would find it hidden away somewhere amongst his papers. He would worry about that later.

He spent the next day looking at computer files and emails, including some from customers. Luckily Ted had been very methodical, allocating a reference number to each new customer, so it was not difficult to find the picture in which they were interested. He phoned an artist by the name of Joe Lampard to tell him he'd sold one of his pictures.

"Edward Howard here," he said

"You're very formal today," Lampard replied, "And what's the matter with your voice?"

Of course, the one thing they hadn't considered was that their voices might sound different!

"I...I've been having throat problems. It's affecting my voice; I think I'll have to see a specialist about it," was all he could come up with.

In all this time he hadn't thought about Ted's death but, suddenly, he had a flashback to him lying in the road with lifeless eyes, and he had a pang of conscience. Not for the first time, he wondered as he looked around him: why had Ted wanted to leave all of this?

That night as he lay in bed, a thought occurred to him; his life insurance.

He had insured his life for a hefty sum; so much so that, when his business declined, he had decided to surrender the policy as an economy measure, but events had put this decision out of his mind. Had he committed suicide, the policy would be invalid, but death in an accident was exactly what it covered; even after clearing his debts, his wife would be a rich woman. Still, why should he begrudge her that? He was well rid of her and starting a comfortable and financially secure new life. With that thought in mind, he fell asleep.

He had just finished breakfast when there was a ring at the door. Using the intercom, he asked who was there, and the reply came,

"Detective Inspector Harrison and Sergeant Ford."

He took them into the sitting room and asked how he could assist them.

"It would help us greatly," said the DI, "If you could tell us where you were, and what you were doing, last Monday evening between 7pm and midnight."

Dave was so taken aback by this question that he nearly said he was at home with his wife, but remembered just in time that he was now Ted Howard.

"I was here, in the flat."

"On your own?"

"Yes."

"What were you doing?"

"I was working – in my office."

"Until midnight?"

"Well…, no, I went to bed about eleven o'clock."

"Did you phone anyone during the evening?"

"No, Inspector, I didn't."

"So you have no means of verifying how you spent that evening?"

Dave was beginning to feel distinctly uneasy.

"I don't know what this is all about. What's the problem, Inspector?"

"Mrs Howard."

He was puzzled for a split second, and then he remembered that, in his new life, she was his ex-wife.

"What about Mrs Howard?"

"I'm sorry to have to tell you that she has been murdered. The assailant pushed a knife into her chest."

Dave felt a constriction in his throat; his new life was going pear-shaped.

He tried to look shocked.

"That is terrible news, how awful. We weren't on the best of terms after the divorce, but she didn't deserve to be murdered. Why should anyone want to kill her?"

"That is precisely what we are trying to ascertain. We think Mrs Howard let her assailant in, as there was no sign of a forced entry, so it seems that she must have known her killer. That is why we need some corroboration as to how you spent Monday evening."

"Well I can't help you, and cannot add anything to what I have already said. I am sorry about Ethel – he was pleased with himself for remembering her first name – but we had very little contact."

The Inspector thanked him, and asked him not to leave town just at present, as he would need to speak to him again very shortly.

When he had gone, Dave broke one of his cardinal rules – never to have an alcoholic drink in the morning – and poured himself a large malt. This was a new and dangerous situation, and he had to think it through very carefully. Everything had been going so well that he had thought there must be a catch, and now came the realisation of what the catch was; Ted had murdered his wife, and that was why he wanted to disappear. He told himself to keep calm, and play it by ear. If the worst came to the worst, he would just have to own up and reveal his true identity.

That afternoon he received more emails from customers but, instead of following them up, he just stared at the screen and, being unable to concentrate, he switched off the computer and had another look through Ted's desk drawers. He found an address book he hadn't seen before, that appeared to be for friends and acquaintances rather than for business purposes. Idly leafing through he came across the words "onto minicab" followed by 140761. A local minicab firm, he thought, but why prefixed by the word "onto"? He puzzled about this and then punched out the number. A voice said, "This number has not been recognised."

Thinking it odd, he dismissed it from his mind; he had other things to worry about.

The next morning the bell rang urgently at six. He answered the door in his, or rather Ted's dressing gown. It was the Inspector, accompanied by two police officers.

"I have a warrant to search your flat," he said, waving it in the air.

Dave sat in a chair as they busied themselves around him. What did they hope to find, he wondered? Eventually they came upon the wall-safe.

"I'd like the combination if you please, Mr Howard," the Inspector said. As he hadn't a clue what the combination was, he did not reply.

"You had better give it to us because, one way or another, we are going to open that safe."

Dave wondered what to do. If he didn't give it to them, they would think he had something to hide. He repeated the word 'combination' to himself and, with a flash of inspiration, realised that it was an anagram of "onto minicab." He particularly remembered the entry in the address book because had the sequence 140761 started with 13, it would have been his date of birth. They opened the safe and found, beneath a pile of documents, a long knife. Dave was arrested and the knife was sent away for forensic examination.

The police found no DNA linking him to the murder, although they analysed samples taken from the scene and a fragment found on the knife. They did have a witness who stated that he saw Ted Howard leaving his wife's house late on that Monday evening. He was a neighbour who knew Howard from the time he was living with Mrs Howard. The police also discovered that she had been demanding money from her ex, and she had been threatening to expose him to the taxman over some creative accounting if he didn't cough up. An identity parade was arranged, and the neighbour picked out Dave Goodman, alias Ted Howard.

Dave knew when the DI walked into the interview room that he was about to be charged, and so he said,

"Before you say anything, I would like to make a statement," and he related the whole story of his meeting with Ted Howard, how they were doubles of each other, and the plan to change identities.

"Very imaginative," the Detective Inspector said.

"I can prove it; my wife, Jean, will know me; let me see her."

They brought Mrs Goodman to the police station, and DI Harrison spoke to her.

"Don't be upset, Mrs Goodman, but we have a man here under arrest in connection with our investigation into the murder of Ethel Howard; he claims to be your husband."

She looked tearful.

"My husband is dead; I had to identify his body in Edinburgh."

"Yes, but he does seem to know you, so perhaps you can tell me whether you have met before."

The DI then ushered her into another room, where Dave was seated. He immediately stood up and walked towards her.

"Jean, thank goodness; tell the Inspector who I am."

Mrs Goodman backed away.

"I don't know you. How did you find out my name? Why are you doing this?"

Her eyes filled with tears, and Dave felt physically sick.

"Of course you know me; I'm your husband, I've lived with you for ten years!"

Mrs Goodman started to cry, and the detective put a comforting arm around her. When she had regained her composure she said,

"I don't know how you found out how long we were married; you have obviously been spying on us, but will you stop this charade? My poor husband died in a road traffic accident - I saw his body."

She turned to the DI.

"This is **too** much; I have to admit there is some similarity in their appearance, but I have never seen this man before."

She produced a photo from her handbag.

"This is my husband."

Dave saw it momentarily before she handed it to the DI. Where on earth had she dug that one up? He thought it had been destroyed; it was one taken some years ago when his hairstyle and colour were different. In those days he also had a moustache, but even then he had thought it did not look like him. Why was she doing this? Of course - the life insurance money! She was a rich woman.

"My husband was a kind man; he wouldn't have put me through an ordeal like this," she said, as Dave lunged at her. The DI grabbed him.

"That's enough," he said, coming between them, and he ushered Mrs Goodman out.